TIME

OF

PROPHECY

K. N. TIMOFEEV

For Nana

ONE

SHE WAS RUNNING for her life through an unfamiliar terrain. In the pitch-black darkness around her, she frantically searched for any familiar landmark or sign of humanity—anything that would save her life from the horror that pursued her.

Her breath was ragged as she ran. The air was thick with humidity and carried with it the scents of stagnant water and heavily perfumed flowers. The contradictory scents were so thick that she could actually taste them on her tongue whenever she opened her mouth.

Branches, brambles, and low-lying brush tore at her limbs and snagged on her clothing as if they, too, wanted to hold her captive in the decaying landscape.

She leaped over a root to only hit a patch of mud that swallowed her foot up to her ankle. With a strangled cry, she pulled her foot free, losing her shoe in the process. Frustration burned the back of her throat as she snatched off her other shoe, throwing it into the dark.

One breath. Two breaths. Three breaths. Get up.

On and on she ran, ignoring the mud, muck, and what have you that squished between her toes. The sticks and stones on the forest floor cut the tender flesh at the bottom of her feet, yet she didn't slow. She didn't dare to. Come what may, she had to make it back to her boat. It was her only chance at surviving this ordeal at all.

After tripping over an unseen root, she closed her eyes and reached for the place where her magic lived. A pale pink light flared to life in the palm of her hand. It wasn't much, but that was the way that she wanted it. She could see her surroundings better, and hopefully, it wasn't strong enough for her pursuer to notice. Waving her hand slowly around, she searched for a clear path to follow. She ignored the shining eyes under the brush and up in the trees. She had nothing to fear from those creatures.

An owl cried out, breaking the silence of the night. The mournful sound sent a shiver down her spine. In some cultures, the owl was the harbinger of death. She sent a quick prayer to the heavens that it wasn't her death the owl called for.

Swallowing down her fear, she sped off in the direction she hoped the river was. She had to get back to town. Not only would the creature chasing her not follow her there, at least for a while, but she would also be able to raise the alarm and call for help.

Without warning, her foot hit another root, and she landed face-first in the mud. Stars danced before her eyes. Her lip busted, and she was left gasping for air until her lungs refilled. Pushing herself up onto all fours, she spat out bits of dirt, grass, and blood. A quick mental examination of her body told her that she hadn't broken or sprained anything in the fall. She breathed a sigh of relief, thanking the gods, her ancestors, and the universe for that small bit of luck.

She struggled to get back to her feet. Her entire body ached and burned. All it wanted to do was stay down in the muck. *Get up. Start moving. Get to the boat.* She gritted her teeth and stumbled back onto her feet. It was then that she realized that every creature that walked, flew, or crawled in the night had vanished or gone silent. The sweat on her body turned to ice as every inch of her tensed, ready to either resume running or to make a stand and fight to the bitter end. She turned around in the clearing, slowly taking in everything that her eyes could glean from the darkness.

Heavy footsteps crashed through the brush behind her. *He* had come. All thoughts of fighting or fleeing vanished from her head. Trembling like an animal caught in a trap, she turned and looked over her shoulder. Her eyes widened as a darkness blacker than anything she had ever seen glided towards her. It seemed to swallow up everything in its path. Plants, animals, light; it didn't matter—all vanished into the darkness and did not return.

Her legs finally gave out beneath her. She lost her entire grip on her magic, and the last vestiges of light faded away. Her fear grew to near-catatonic levels when the darkness enveloped her, cutting her off from the natural world around her. She couldn't even feel the ground beneath her.

Suddenly, a blinding white skull soared through the darkness straight for her. Its eyes burned with an unholy fire that could have only come from the deepest pits of hell. The fire carried with it the promise to consume her very essence and a great amount of pain.

She began to cry. She had failed. She would die tonight, and no one will ever know why or who did it. They probably wouldn't even find her body.

The skull descended upon her. She did the only thing that was left for her to do—scream.

Erin was wrenched from her sleep, gripping the edges of her desk white-knuckled and drenched in sweat. Her eyes rapidly scanned her surroundings. The frantic beating of her heart slowed as she looked about the space. She wasn't in a swamp. She was safe and sound in the Grand Library at the same desk she had settled into hours before. Scattered on the floor around her were her notes on a ritual she was helping to translate.

She took several deep breaths, but there was something about that nightmare that still bothered her. She could still feel the muggy kiss of the warm air on her skin, could still smell the decay. It was almost like she had been there or at least experienced it through another's eyes.

As she continued to breathe, she caught a whiff of smoke. The nightmare, vision, whatever it was, had scared her so deeply that she had summoned magic in her sleep. The desk now bore several scorch marks about the size of her hand. She wrapped her arms around her body as she pulled her knees into her chest. She had never done that before. She stared at the scorched desk, semi-lost in the aftereffects of what she witnessed. The nightmare felt too real to be anything other than an actual event. Someone had been hunted down like an animal.

Erin was so wrapped up in her own thoughts that she didn't even hear Orrin walk up behind her. She nearly jumped out of her skin when he spoke.

"I know you take your job as Guardian seriously," Orrin said with a frown, "but you'll be no good for anyone if you don't start taking better care of yourself. Don't make me have to set up a curfew." His stern expression cracked as he fought to restrain a smirk. When he noticed Erin's haunted expression, however, his laughter died. "What happened?"

Erin shook her head. She wasn't ready to talk about it yet. The vision was too fresh, too raw in her mind to speak about it for fear of bringing it to her.

Orrin clenched his jaw, respecting Erin's wishes. He knelt to gather the book and papers from the floor. When he placed them on the desk, he noticed the scorch marks and chewed the inside of his cheek in irritation.

"Well, if you're going to turn into a human candle every time you take a nap, please do so on the stone flooring. These desks *are* antiques, you know?"

His joke finally broke through the haze left over from the vision. Erin let out a breathy laugh, rolling her eyes. "I'll try to keep that in mind," she joked, uncurling from her chair.

She swayed, suddenly overcome with exhaustion. Orrin was right; she needed to rest.

She stretched, letting out a satisfied noise when her back popped and crackled, releasing some tension. Though her eyes burned from a lack of sleep, she was reluctant to leave the Library. She closed her eyes and listened, nothing other than the ticking of a clock somewhere in the distance. The energy in the Library was sleepy and peaceful, vastly different from how it felt during the day when dozens, if not hundreds, of people combed through the shelves.

Orrin reopened the Grand Library as soon as he felt like he had a handle on his new status as Head Librarian. Once the word got out, they were flooded with requests. Families that were nearly extinct pleaded for their family's collection of spells and charms to be added to the Library's vast collection, therefore ensuring that their legacies live on in some manner. Those new to magic clamored for access to the wealth of knowledge stored within the hallowed walls. There were even some families who hoped that their family's lost books may have found their way into the Library.

It was almost too much for Orrin and Erin to handle, but they made it work. Orrin granted access to all, regardless of their lineage. He, like Erin, believed that if their world was to continue to survive, they would need to let go of the trappings of the past. Erin handled the witchlings, those who were just learning about magic. She guided them through the basics as best she could since she was still new to magic herself. She loved it, and she even began to make new friends. Each friend became an ally that she could call upon if and when she needed a little extra power.

The first of Erin's new acquaintances were a pair of eclectic hedge witches. These two middle-aged women were a force to be reckoned with. They were quick to put someone in their place, yet they were exceedingly gentle with the witchlings. Erin loved them right off the bat.

Then there was the small but proud magical family. Their lineage wasn't as impressive as the older families, but they were determined to help Erin reshape their world into one of equality and peace.

Her latest ally was a solitary practitioner who had traveled all the way from Paris just to meet her. Through him, Erin and Orrin hoped to establish a few lines of communication to the wider world of magic users.

So much had changed in a short amount of time, and in that time, Erin found a sense of peace. Her vision brought her crashing back to the reality that she was supposed to be preparing for a war that may or may not happen in her lifetime. Perhaps the vision was a sign that the battle her ancestor Kieran had foreseen so many centuries ago was finally about to happen. Erin secretly hoped that it was. She knew that it was un-Guardian-like of her to have such thoughts, but she *hated* the waiting, *hated* the not knowing. Waiting grated on her nerves. She wanted the whole ordeal over and done with, no matter if she won or lost.

Erin mentally growled because Connor, once again, had retreated to wherever he went to hatch his wicked schemes. She couldn't find him and neither could any of her allies. There was nothing left for her to do but study and add to her ever-growing arsenal of spells and potions for when she finally met Connor on the field of battle—if and whenever that happened. Although no one else in her family seemed too keen on speeding up the prophecy.

Erin rubbed the back of her neck and made a frustrated noise. Sometimes she missed the days when she knew nothing about magic or the prophecy that hung over her family. She slowly shook her head, pulling out a golden chain from beneath her shirt. At the end of the chain rested an ordinary-looking skeleton key. Though it didn't look like anything special, it was an extremely powerful magic tool. The key gave the owner instant and unrestricted access to the Grand Library. So far, only Orrin and Erin had keys.

Orrin studied his friend intently. "Are you sure you're OK?"

"Yeah, I'm sorry," Erin said, waving his concern off. "I guess I've been pushing myself too hard lately. It was just a nightmare. Nothing to worry about." The last part she said more for her benefit than Orrin's.

Orrin made a skeptical noise, not believing a word Erin said.

"I'm not entirely sure what happened," she amended. "I had a dream, but it seemed too real … I'm not quite sure what to make of it." She chewed on her thumb, lost in thought.

"I'm here for you for whatever you need," Orrin promised, clasping her shoulder.

Erin gave him a brief nod and attempted a smile before she headed towards the nearest door. She pulled the chain over her head and slid the key into place. She closed her eyes, focusing on where she wanted to go—home. She turned the key, and the doorframe began to glow. She removed the key, stringing it back around her neck, reaching for the doorknob at the same time. The light around the border of the door disappeared when she turned the knob and pushed the door open.

Instead of walking into a dark earthen tunnel, Erin crossed the threshold of her house, several miles away. A smile broke out across her face the moment her feet touched the thick, colorful rug that ran from the door straight up the stairs that stood in front of the door. In the months following the discovery of her family's secret lineage, the house had gone from a place to lay her head to the foundation of her stability.

Frantic yowling heralded the arrival of a small white cat with red ears. Erin smiled at her constant companion and closest friend, Fae the fairy cat. Her smile faltered the closer the petite feline got. His fur was raised from the nape of his neck to his ramrod straight tail. Somehow, some way, he knew. He knew what Erin saw, and it had agitated him just as much.

Fae stopped at the foot of the stairs, his eyes glowing bright green. "What happened?" he demanded. "I felt yer fear. I felt the power of the land surge up to yer call."

Erin slowly hung her coat on a hook by the door. She walked into the kitchen followed hotly by Fae. She placed her bag on her kitchen table. She pulled out a chair and sat down. Fae leaped from the floor to the table. They sat eye to eye, tension heavy in the air around them. The dreadful truth of her vision crashed over her like a tidal wave. She wanted to deny it. Her body recoiled at the implications.

Fiddling with the end of her hair, Erin finally spoke the words she had been too afraid to say in the Grand Library. "I think ..." She closed her eyes and swallowed back the terror rising in her throat. "I think something has happened to my family. I think one of us has fallen into enemy hands."

"Who?"

She knew that simple word meant so much more. Who was taken? Who is behind it?

"I don't know," Erin replied. Goosebumps sprang up on her arms. She tried to rub them away. "I need to call mom ... Gran ... someone."

Erin pushed away from the table. Each step towards the phone felt like an eternity. Each step cleared away her frantic and erratic thoughts. She knew. She saw. She understood. She punched in a number and then listened for the other person to pick up.

"What happened to Laura?" Erin demanded the moment she heard the connection.

Her mother's voice cracked and wavered. "For extra credit, Laura signed up to help rebuild homes along the bayous in some rural part of Louisiana. Before she went, she told me that she wanted to do this because that's what our family was supposed to do—help people. At first, everything was going well. She enjoyed the work and fell in love with the area where they worked. But then ..."

"Then what?"

"But then, strange things, accidents began to happen. Laura suspected that all the accidents came from a magical source. I told her to not go off on her own, but she's just as stubborn as you."

A reluctant smile tugged a corner of Erin's mouth. "Was she right?"

Erin heard her mother cry on the other end of the phone. "I don't know. She disappeared a week ago. The local police only just told me this morning." The last vestiges of her mother's composure evaporated. Erin listened in growing sickening horror as her mother's gut-wrenching, heart-rendering sobs echoed in her ears.

Her beloved sister who marched to the beat of her own drum, not giving a damn about what anyone else thought of her; her sister whose heart was bigger and gentler than anyone else Erin had ever known was missing. Tears prickled her eyes, and her throat tightened. The vision she had earlier took on a new horrifying reality. Her sister could be … Erin shook her head, dispelling the dark thoughts. She couldn't think like that. Whether it was her sisterly intuition or a byproduct of her familial lineage, she knew that Laura wasn't dead. And as long as her sister lived, there was a chance for her to be rescued.

Erin gripped the telephone tightly, swallowing down her fear and desperation. "I'm coming back," she said. The other end of the line fell silent.

"No!" her mother shouted, "You are safest where you are. My mother and I will take care of it."

Erin shook her head. "I may be, but Laura isn't. Someone went after her. I'm sure of it."

"Have you seen something?" Her mother's voice took on a steely edge that Erin hadn't thought her to be capable of.

"I had a vision where I was Laura. I was chased through a swamp by someone that I couldn't see." Erin chewed her thumb, thinking back on the vision and what her mother had told her. "I think Laura has been taken by a dark practitioner. I think someone is trying to lure me out of the safety of my territory."

"All the more reason for you to stay where you are," her mother protested.

"I can't, mom," Erin said with a sigh. "It's my job as head of this family to look after its members. How can I call myself a Guardian when I can't even protect my own family?"

Silence on the other end of the line. Erin felt her mother reluctantly bend to her will. "Do you need money for the plane ticket?"

"No, I'm straight," Erin replied. "I'll call you later when I have all the details. Until then, fortify the wards around your house and have Gran do the same. I don't want anything to happen to either of you."

"You should take your own advice," her mother quipped back.

"I will, I promise. See you soon, mom. I love you."

"I love you more. Stay safe."

"I will."

Erin hung up the phone, reeling from the night's revelations. Her sister gone, the trap laid out for her, all of it. A chill ran down her spine, causing her to shiver uncontrollably. Erin closed her eyes and took several calming breaths in an attempt to center her mind and focus. She had far too much to do in too short a time. She sighed and picked up the phone again. She had several calls to make if she was going to run back to the country of her birth in search of her lost sister.

Once again, Erin was seated on a midnight flight with her emotions ripped to shreds. The only difference from the last time was that this time, her trip was a rescue mission and not an escape. Still, it felt strange for her to be returning back to America. When she fled from her abusive husband a year and a half ago, she never thought that she would ever step foot there again. Her mind reeled at how much her life had changed in such a short span of time. But looking back, she wouldn't have changed anything about her past. It was her past that had shaped her into the person she was today, pain and all, and she liked who she was.

A stewardess pushes a squeaky cart down the narrow aisle, offering refreshments before the flight gets underway. "Can I offer you anything, ma'am?"

"Got any of those tiny liquor bottles?" Erin asked, rubbing her hands nervously over her knees. She could see the disapproval on the stewardess' face but didn't give a damn. She needed something to take the edge off, something that would maybe help her get a few hours of rest. The stewardess handed over a tiny bottle and a small cup with ice with pursed lips. Erin ignored the cup and tipped the bottle back. She handed it back before leaning back into her seat, with her eyes closed. The alcohol burned her mouth and throat but did nothing to chase away her anxiety.

"Nervous flier?" asked a gentle voice beside her.

Erin cracked open an eye. An old man sat next to her, smiling kindly. "Not really," she answered, closing her eyes once again. "Just got a lot going on."

"Well, make sure you take this time to get a little rest. Whatever is going on won't be any better or worse until you get there."

Erin exhaled sharply through her nose and bit back her retort. The old man was just trying to be helpful. That was no reason to bite his head off. It also helped that he was right. She would be no good to anyone if she was too exhausted to think straight, but try as she might, her mind would not shut off. Her body would not relax. Even when the sky around her darkened, and the cabin was filled with the sounds of sleeping people, Erin sat wide awake. When she wasn't worrying about how to save her sister from her faceless, nameless foe, she fretted over all the loose ends she left dangling in the wind when she fled across the ocean the first time. Would she run into some of her old friends? What would they think of her now? What about John?

Surely, he wouldn't still be hanging around. What if he was
…? Erin threw her head back with a groan. At this rate, she
would never fall asleep.

Another stewardess makes her rounds. Erin got two
more bottles. She needed sleep. She tossed both back,
coughing slightly. Both her throat and her eyes burned.
She propped her head against the hard wall of the plane,
relying on its unyielding and rough nature to keep her
grounded in the physical world as she fell into a fitful
slumber.

Perhaps her ancestors were looking out for her.
Perhaps the alcohol prevented it. Or perhaps she had
reached that level of exhaustion that left the body incapable
of doing anything else but to fall into a deep void of
existence, but the vision did not appear for a second
showing.

Erin slept like the dead for the entire flight. She
only woke when the stewardesses ordered everyone to return
their trays to the upright position and for them to buckle up.
Erin complied before turning her attention to the horizon.
Her eyes strained to see beyond the horizon line all the way
to Louisiana.

Please hold on, Laura, Erin silently urged her sister, pulling hard on the invisible threads that bound them together. *I'm coming for you. Hold on just a little bit longer.*

Two

I T'S FUNNY HOW once familiar surroundings can change yet stay exactly the way you remember them. Erin took in the once familiar sites from the window of the taxi, lost in the haze of memory. So many places, so many smells, all dredging up long-forgotten memories of her past; many she never wanted to live through again. And yet for all the ghosts that in and out of her consciousness, nothing she saw outside the taxi cab window felt like home. It was then that she realized that this land of glittering lights and impressive structures *was* no longer her home. Her home was thousands of miles away, nestled in a sleepy little village of crumbling buildings and rolling pastures where the land sang a special melody just for her. Just thinking of Dorshire brought a smile to her face and provided a sense of comfort that she desperately needed to get through the night like a balm to a burn.

In the silence of the cab, a familiar tune began to play softly through the radio. Erin struggled to place the music since it was nothing she had ever heard on any radio station, and she didn't remember the cabbie turning the radio on. She closed her eyes and listened.

The harder she strained her ears, the clearer the melody became. It filled her mind's eye with images of crackling hearths in bitter winter storms; of soft rains filling the air with the scent of rich, fertile earth; of fragrant breezes cooling sweat kissed skin. Her eyes flew open in surprise. It was the song of Dorshire. She had heard the melody only once before, when she had accepted her role as Guardian. Erin smiled and leaned back, letting the music wash over her. Woven into the song was a message. The message was that no matter how far she traveled, there would always be a place for her to return to, a place that was as much a part of her as she was of it.

The scenery changed as the ride progressed. Fast food chains replaced by smaller shops and upscale restaurants. Apartment complexes became neighborhoods, and then impressive mansions. The streets got quieter and quieter until the only vehicle on the road was the cab Erin rode in. The closer to her childhood home she got, the more she felt her body curve inward in an attempt to protect herself from the feeling of hallowedness that echoed in every cold corner. Her inner fire sputtered and dimmed. She felt like an animal being led to a cage—a cage where she would be forced to give up her individuality to fit into a mold that she didn't want, never wanted; a cage where every last little bit of her would be scrubbed away until she was ...

No!

Erin recoiled from that particular train of thought. There was no one here who could hurt her, not now. There was no one who could make her do anything that she didn't want to do. She may have left this place broken nearly beyond repair, but she has been reforged and was stronger than ever before. She also wasn't alone in the world like last time. She had her mother and grandmother to back her up ... and her sister once she was found. Erin jutted her chin forward defiantly. She would show the shadows of her past just how much she had changed in the time she had been gone.

The taxi stopped at last in front of a tall brick wall with an iron gate. Not a single bit of foliage hung over the top, neither did a single vine of ivy grow up the sides. Another stark difference between Erin's old life and the new one she had forged for herself across the sea.

"All right, little lady, here we are. That will be thirty-five dollar even."

Erin handed the cash to the cabbie and got out, using her hands to stretch out the lower portion of her back. She threw the strap of her duffel bag over her shoulder while the cabbie got her suitcase out of the trunk. She only brought one. She had filled it with a mixture of the mundane and the magical. When she packed, she had been a little worried about making it through customs, but no one batted an eye.

The cabbie got back into his vehicle with a "goodnight" and sped off into the night in hopes of another fare, leaving Erin to face the hardest leg of her journey.

It was difficult for Erin to take the few steps towards the keypad that would let her through the gate. So many different emotions whirled around in her mind that she wasn't quite sure how she felt.

Regret, shame, fear, and all the other emotions she had once been well acquainted with all clamored for control of her mind like wolves howling for the kill. Fortunately, she was able to shove the wolves back into the darkness where they belonged and strode towards the gate with her head held high. She punched in a series of numbers that had been the same as when she lived within the walls.

The gate swung open without a sound as lights flared to life up the driveway. It was a long walk up to the main house. She sighed, resigned and adjusted the strap of her duffle bag, extended the handle to her suitcase and walked through the gate for the first time in over three years.

As she trudged up the long driveway, she wondered about her father. She never asked her mom how he handled her sister's disappearance or how he handled hers for that matter. She wondered if he would yell and shout at her, cry and embrace her, or completely ignore her. *Most likely the latter,* she thought. It wasn't that her father didn't love them; he just didn't know how to show his emotions. More often than not he would hide away in his office, pretending that the problems of his family either didn't exist or could be solved by acquiring more money, more prestige. Oh, how little did he know about the people in his life!

Gravel crunched under her feet and the wheels of her suitcase as she slowly made her way up the driveway. Her breath became ragged, but she didn't stop. She was a little embarrassed at how tired this little walk was making her. She swore to get back into the gym as soon as she rescued her sister from whatever trouble she had managed to get herself into.

For some unknown reason, Erin's instincts urged her to keep to the shadows. The feeling confused her; this was her parents' home, her childhood home. Why would she need to stay in the shadows? Her mother was expecting her. Even though she couldn't discern the reasoning behind the feeling, she complied. If her instincts urged caution, then that is what she would do. They haven't led her astray yet.

Sweat beaded along her forehead and along her spine by the time her parents' house came into view. Erin paused to take in her former home, breathing slightly harder than she cared to admit. Her brows furrowed at the sight of dozens of cars lined the circled driveway and the lights that shone in every window. Her confusion turned to anger when she heard music faintly from somewhere within the depths of the impressive mansion.

Erin seethed and bared her teeth. She could not believe what she saw. Her parents were hosting a *party* while her sister was *missing*! The blood in her veins turned into a fiery river that grew and grew until it threatened to take over her completely. Magic shimmered at her fingertips in response to that fire, sparkling like the ends of fuses. Erin was a bomb set to detonate.

She marched straight to the front door, power pulsating beneath her skin with each step. Her power filled her until she felt like an overripe piece of fruit ready to burst. The rational portions of her mind compelled her to regain her composure and control her magic, not the other way around, or she will inadvertently kill everyone inside her parents' house. A sliver of calm carved its way through the raging inferno in her blood. Erin latched onto that calm, expelling the excess energy with several calming breaths. When she was at last filled with nothing else but herself, she turned the doorknob and crossed the threshold of her childhood home for the first time in many years.

Everything was exactly how Erin remembered it. The mosaic flooring still shone with freshly laid wax, the colors still as vibrant as the day they were first laid down. Right in the middle of the floor was a large section of tile that boasted a large gilded letter, the first letter of her father's family name. Dual staircases followed the curved room in graceful arches towards the second story. Even now, they made her think of the numerous fairy tales her mother read to her and her sister when they were little. The house did have an actual ballroom. It was a little further ahead, through a set of gilded French doors. It had been built like an octagon with a glass ceiling so that the occupants could marvel at the stars or watch the snow fall.

Just off the ballroom would be the gourmet kitchen that her mother had renovated when she first married Erin's father. It was her pride and joy.

The rest of the house's layout flowed through Erin's mind. Just through the darkened doorway to her right were the main living areas. There was a formal dining room where her mother hosted many a dinner as well as a smaller, more intimate dining room used for daily family meals. The family room sat near the front of the house, although it was only used during the holidays since her family was often too busy to mingle with each other. To her left was her father's study that connected to the billiard room. She couldn't recall *ever* stepping foot into either room. Although she did have fond memories of evenings spent curled up in an overstuffed chair reading in the expansive library. It was in the library where she often hid from her mother's overbearing but well-meaning friends—who were so intent on Erin and Laura dating their sons, all of whom were the worst example of privileged youths.

All the bedrooms and bathrooms were on the upper levels of the house. Erin and Laura both had their own room, plus an *en suite* bathroom, *plus* another room to house their various interests and awards. The second floor also boasted several guest rooms, each one artfully and carefully decorated of course.

There was also another study on the second floor that Erin and her sister used. It clashed terribly with the rest of the house because they had wanted to make a space for themselves with their own styles. Erin's parents had their own space at the other end of the house, furthest away from the hustle and bustle of the rest of the house. Erin and her sister never once in all their lives ventured into their parents' territory.

The grounds on which the house sat were as equally impressive as the house itself. Her great-grandfather had purchased the largest parcel of land available on which to build his estate. He wanted to have a buffer between himself and the rest of the world. Her grandmother had spent her entire married life turning the rolling hills behind the manor house into a garden that would have made the Queen jealous.

When Erin turned eight, her father added an Olympic sized pool to the backyard for some reason. As far as she could remember, not one person in her family ever swam in it. Their lives had been too hectic for such luxuries.

Everything within the walls and without had once been the norm for Erin, but now her life was completely different, simpler. Growing up, she never liked all the pomp and circumstance that went along with having a house like this, but it made her mother and grandmother happy. She shrugged her shoulders and headed towards where the party was taking place. She knew that would be the best place to find her mother. Her mother was never happier than when she was entertaining and making other people happy.

Erin dropped her bag by the left staircase. There was nothing more that she wanted than to fall face-first into a soft mattress now that her anger had abated a bit, but first, she needed to see her mother to quiet the portion of her mind that feared that something new had happened while she had been in transit.

No one took notice of her as she entered the ballroom. She hadn't expected them to. Dozens of fancily dressed people milled about the ballroom talking and eating. In a small corner of the room, a four-string quartet played quietly, seemingly invisible to the party goers. The same could be said of the men and women wearing black vests that carried silver trays filled with horderves and champagne. None of the faces in the crowd were familiar to Erin. Finding her mother may be harder than she thought. Maneuvering through the crowd was the last thing she wanted to do tonight. Thankfully, she had a magical solution to her predicament.

Erin closed her eyes and opened her mind, searching for a familiar red thread—the thread that connected Erin to her family. When she located the thread that connected her to her mother, she sent a silent message down it. She told her mother that she was home and to meet her in the garden just outside the ballroom as soon as she could detangle herself from her guests.

A hand grasped her shoulder roughly, spinning her around. It startled Erin so much that her mind went blank and a gasp escaped from her mouth. The surprise on her face lingered when she came face to face with the scowling face of her father.

Her father hadn't changed much from the last time she'd seen him, which had been the first time she had left her abusive husband. He still had the same shrewd eyes, the same mixture of hazel as hers. Though he still stood straight and tall, he had started to lose the youthful zeal of his frame. Once she saw that, her eyes were open to the other subtle changes to her father. The lines around his eyes and mouth were deeper as if he spent more time frowning than smiling these days. His hair had taken on more gray than she remembered, and he no longer gave off an aura of endless energy. Instead, her father seemed tired as if he bore the weight of the world on his shoulders.

Erin's father stared deeply into her eyes, searching for something. His scowl softened, taking on a completely different emotion. One Erin had never seen before—love.

"Erin." He whispered her name as softly as a prayer. Before she could formulate a thought, he pulled her into a tight embrace. One of his hands went up to cradle the back of her head while the other pulled her in close. Erin was too stunned by such a public display of affection that she froze.

"There are no words that can express how sorry I am for not being there when you needed me the most. I have failed you as a father. It's my job to protect you from those who would hurt you. Can you ever forgive me?"

Shocked, Erin pulled away from her father. Her face grew warm. Hurt filled his eyes while smoldering embers sparked in hers. Did he honestly think that it would only take a couple of sweet words to mend the chasm between them? "This isn't something you can fix overnight," she told him, crossing her arms.

Her father's face morphed again, mirroring the anger on his eldest daughter's face. "I am *your father*. The only one you will ever have in this life. We are family, and family sticks together, no matter what."

His voice cracked and wavered, but to Erin, it was all a façade. Her barely checked frustration threatened to boil over.

"The same kind of family that has a party while one of its members is *missing*." Erin took another step back, increasing the distance between them. Her voice became a razor's edge. "Do you even care … about any of us?"

Her father threw his shoulders back, towering over Erin. She knew that he was attempting to assert his dominance over her, but it didn't work. She had faced situations and foes far deadlier than her father in a temper. She and her father had always bashed head when they argued. They were both too dominating, too much like each other to ever coexist in peace. Like so many times in the past, Erin's mother, Jessica, swooped in before the standoff could come to blows.

"Senator Cromwell has been looking for you all night, darling," her mother cooed, steering her husband away from her daughter. "I think he wanted to talk to you about that land deal."

Erin's dad gave her one last cold stare before disappearing into the crowd. Her mother exhaled, her shoulders sagging in relief. Erin remained tense, poised for a fight. She snatched two glasses of bubbling champagne from a passing server, throwing both back before handing them back to the stunned server. The drink tasted delicious, sweet, with a hint of something harsher at the end. Perhaps drinking two back to back wasn't the best idea.

"You know how your father is," her mother said, her voice soft and calming. "You know he plunges into his work whenever he's upset. Your grandfather was much the same way ... not that that excuses him ..." she added, quickly throwing her hands up, seeing the glare on Erin's face. "Can't you cut him a little slack?"

Erin sighed, shoulders slumping. Her body demanded food and rest. Her eyes burned with exhaustion. The two drinks she tossed back had created a pool of liquid fire in her stomach. It was completely different from the fire she felt earlier. This one warmed her body like a hot bath, stealing away the last fragments of her strength. All she wanted was a bed. She didn't think she would last much longer, but she had a few things to attend to first before losing herself to sleep.

"Have there been any news?"

Her mother's face fell, and she started to pick at her carefully manicured nails. She tried to give Erin a reassuring smile, but it fell flat. She lightly steered Erin towards the bar where Erin took a seat and waited for her to fill her in. The bartender placed two glasses of whiskey with knuckles worth of amber liquid each. A small sandwich accompanied one of the glasses. Erin dug in, knowing that her mother wouldn't continue until she had eaten something. Her mother watched her with dull, vacant eyes.

Erin bit into the sandwich. She wasn't sure what it was made of, but whatever it was, it was delicious. Her eyes nearly rolled into the back of her head in ecstasy. She opened her eyes and took another bite, motioning for her mother to go on.

"No."

The sandwich turned to ash in Erin's mouth.

Her mother plowed ahead. "The local authorities have no idea where Laura is or what may have caused her to vanish. It's nearly driven me mad. I have half a mind to go down there and set a fire under their asses—metaphorically and physically." The corner of Erin's mouth twitched. Her mother took a deep breath to regain her composure. "I know you want to help," Erin's mother said, turning to her, "but do you think it's a good idea for you to be here? What about the house? What about the war with Connor and his vulgar family?"

Erin gave her mother what she hoped was a reassuring smile. "I took precautions when I left. And as for Connor, I haven't seen or heard anything for months." She took a swig of her drink, holding the burning liquid in her mouth for as long as she could stand before swallowing.

She took a deep breath that mirrored her mother's and told her mother about her vision, not sparing a single detail. At the end of Erin's story, both women signaled the bartender for another round of drinks.

"There's nothing that I can do from across the world," Erin stated as she swirled her drink around in her glass. "I have to go to Louisiana. It's our best chance at finding Laura. You and Gran can stay here and keep an eye out for any other signs of trouble."

Her mother gasped and snatched up Erin's hand, nearly crushing her fingers. "No, I won't allow it."

Erin placed her hand on top of her mother's, her face solemn. "There's no other way. That's the reason why I had that vision, not you or Gran."

Her mother closed her eyes. Her answer was in a resigned voice, "You two were always close as children."

Erin nodded. "That's right. We share a bond, and it's through that bond that I intend to find her. But first, I'll talk to the local police. Laura's been missing for a while, so my arrival wouldn't appear too out of place. I'll conduct my own investigation. But is there anything Laura mentioned to you that you haven't told the police, anything possibly *magic* in nature?"

Erin's mother pondered, resting her chin on her hand. She opened her mouth to answer but stopped when Erin's face cracked open with a huge yawn. Whatever her mother had been about to say was lost to motherly concern.

"You won't do anyone a bit of good if you drop dead from exhaustion. Go to bed and get some rest. We'll talk in the morning. Your grandmother was coming later on, and I think it's best if the *three* of us make a plan. You may be the one in charge when it comes to the magical aspects of our family, but when it comes to the more mundane aspects of our family, I am the head."

Erin shook her head and let out a small laugh. She knew better than to argue with her mother on this matter. She dutifully swore to save all heroic rescues for later and finished her drink in record time. The alcohol made her head swim and amplified just how tired she was. She really could use a few hours of sleep before she hit the road again. They turned to leave the bar. Across the room, Erin met a pair of ice blue eyes that she was well acquainted with.

Connor smiled at her from across the ballroom, giving her a mocking bow.

"What the hell!" Erin snarled, adrenaline kicking in.

Erin felt her mother tense beside her. Her mother's hand slipped into hers, though it was not for comfort. If Connor wanted to throw down, they would have to pull on their combined strength to fight him. For a brief moment, Erin wished she was back in Dorshire. At least there they would have the home field advantage that came in the form of protection by her bloodline. *Protection from her bloodline,* an interesting choice of words. Erin kept her face neutral, betraying nothing. She had an idea, a reckless, preposterous idea, but an idea nonetheless. Perhaps luck would be on her side.

"He shouldn't be here," Erin's mother snarled softly at her side. Erin felt a flash of pride as she felt her mother shift into an inconspicuous fighting stance and the smooth, steady pulse of magic that came from her. "I've been severing all his connections to your father for months. I like to know how the bastard found out about this party in the first place."

Connor flashed a brilliant smile at the women before blending into the crowd like the oily serpent he was. Erin's scowl deepened. She sucked on her teeth as she rolled her neck and shoulders. "Go to dad as fast as you can!" she ordered her mom.

Her mother inclined her head slightly before weaving her way through the crowd towards her husband. The two women were no longer mother and daughter. They were a subordinate following a direct order from the head of her family.

Erin remained where she stood, scanning the crowd to see where Connor had slithered off to. She spotted him near the entrance to the ballroom. Connor flashed another smile before walking out of the ballroom.

Keep smiling, prick, Erin sneered, *I got something that will wipe that smirk off your face.*

Erin turned on her heel and wove through the crowd as graceful as a dancer in the opposite direction Connor went. She paid no attention to the glittering people around her, and they ignored her too, for the most part. The few that did notice Erin's progression felt a chill run down their spine at the intense and predatory gleam in her eyes. They sent a silent prayer to the heavens for the unlucky soul who would be at the receiving end of her fiery gaze.

Erin pushed through a set of swinging doors and left behind the glittering world of the ballroom for the barely controlled chaos in the kitchen. Heat caressed her body like a gentle lover as her forehead broke out into a sweat. All around her, the kitchen staff dashed about, performing their tasks with a military precision. A few glanced at Erin from the corner of their eyes, but none made a move to stop her as she walked through the kitchen. She snatched bits of food from various trays, woofing them down without savoring their rich flavors and delicate textures. She snatched an unattended water bottle, chugging it quickly before tossing it into a nearby bin.

Fortified by food, drink, and a half-baked idea, Erin dove deep into the well pool of her power, drawing on a strength she rarely needed to call upon. Her bones hummed from the raw energy. The hairs on her arms and the back of her neck rose. As she passed open flames, they burned hotter and brighter until she passed. Just before she walked out of the kitchen, she grabbed a small knife left unattended on the counter; it was nothing more than a peering knife, but it was sharp and would serve her purpose.

Walking through another set of swinging doors, Erin left the chaotic world of the kitchen behind her. She lingered in the darkness, safe and protected. Once her eyes adjusted to the shadows around her, she maneuvered around the large dining table where her mother hosted many a dinner party. She trailed a hand over an ornate chair. Lights sparked to life along the tips of her fingers. She walked through an ornate doorway and entered the more casual family dining room. Erin smiled softly as memories of better days sitting around the circular table filled her thoughts. She latched onto those thoughts to help strengthen her resolve. If she failed, all those memories would be lost—forever.

With one last fortifying breath, Erin left the safety of the shadows and strode purposely into the foyer, blinking against the bright lights. She palmed the peering knife against her sweaty palm. Her steps echoed strong and steady in the silence of the room. With each step, she pushed her uncertainty and fear deep down. She could not afford to give those feelings any ground lest she succumb to their crippling power.

"Come now," Connor taunted, standing near the center of the room. "There's no need to look so grim." Erin stopped a few feet shy of him before the ornate symbol of her family's name. His voice held a cruel teasing edge to it. "I don't bite unless asked." He flashed a cocky smile that sent her stomach rolling.

Erin rolled her eyes. "What are you doing here? What do you want, Connor?"

Connor attempted and failed to twist his face into a mask of hurt. The dark light behind his icy eyes gave away his cruel delight in causing discomfort. "My dear Erin, you wound me. Have we not begun to forge the bonds of friendship due to our *similar abilities*?"

"Cut the crap," Erin snapped, crossing her arms, jutting her hip to the side. Her teeth ached from how hard she clenched them. Her whole body quivered as a taut bowstring, ready to lash out at a moment's notice.

Connor's ever-present smirk took on a darker undertone that raised goose bump along Erin's body. "When I first laid eyes on you, my darling, you were utterly ignorant of your true powers and potential. That is no longer the case." His eyes roamed over her body. She resisted the urge to shudder under his presumptuous gaze. "You've grown beautifully into your powers. You've even managed to surprise me, a first and certainly the last. We both know that we are nearing the inevitable. It is time and past for our families to settle the long-standing score between us. I recommend you do it sooner rather than later or more innocent lives will be lost."

From his pocket, Connor pulled out a necklace that turned Erin's blood to ice. She recognized it the moment she saw the pendant swing in the light. It was the necklace her sister chose as her heirloom, the conduit in which she could call on the powers of their ancestors. There was only one way Connor could have gotten possession of it.

"If you harm one hair on her head," Erin snarled, slipping into a fighting stance, "I will eradicate every part of you!"

Connor beamed like a spoiled child getting his way. "How wonderfully violent of you; not at all what one would expect a benevolent *Guardian* would say at all."

"Everyone has their breaking point."

"I'm counting on that."

Erin narrowed her eyes. "You have five seconds to tell me where Laura is and leave my parents' house before I kick your pompous ass from here back to Ireland."

Connor threw his head back and roared in laughter. "You don't have the power to back up those words, darling. In case you have forgotten, *this* house isn't protected by your interfering ancestors. You can no more bar me from this house than you can stop the wind from blowing where it will."

Erin eased her stance, plastering a sharp smile of her own on her face. "You forget, *my good sir*, that there is more than one bloodline that flows through my veins. This house was built by my grandfather and has passed from father to son on my *father's* side, the side that never likes to play by the rules and who always pushes the boundaries of what can be done. I get just as much from him as I do my mother."

Erin quickly slashed the blade of the peering knife across the palm of her hand. It hurt worse than she expected, but still, she kept that harsh smile on her face. She tossed the knife aside. It clattered across the floor, splattering droplets of blood. Erin raised her bleeding hand and clenched it tight, encouraging her blood to flow faster. Her eyes took on an otherworldly gleam as she called on ancient powers to sanctify her parents' home against those who would harm them. Words spoken in a long-forgotten language poured out of her mouth, echoing as if a multitude of people were speaking at once. The lights flickered as magic filled the space.

Connor stood frozen, not fully believing what was unfolding in front of him.

"It appears I have surprised you a second time," Erin sneered. "Continue to underestimate me, please. Now GET OUT!" she shouted as she slammed her bloody palm on the ornate letter in the middle of the floor.

Magic erupted, rolling out from the circle in waves. With each pulse, lights flickered, and the doors and windows rattled. The front door was flung open by an unseen, unfelt wind. Connor regained his composure in time to glare daggers at Erin before an invisible force lifted him off the floor and flung him unceremoniously out the front door. The open door closed with a resounding bang as the magic fused with everything that was tied to her father's family, creating a safety net of protection just like her home in Dorshire.

As the magic settled down, Erin swayed on her feet. She barely registered her knees hitting the floor as her legs gave out. Stars danced before her eyes while the edges of her vision darkened. *I over exhorted myself again*, she thought numbly as she fell to the floor and her world went black.

The clacking of high heels on the hard floor brought Erin back from the darkness, barely. Her mother raced across the room, panic clear on her face. Erin tried to open her mouth to assure her mother that she was fine, but her body wouldn't respond; her mind couldn't find the words.

"Erin," her mother cried, falling to the floor beside her daughter. A lavender light sparkled around the hand she pressed against Erin's sweaty brow. Erin leaned into the soothing touch, and she heard her mother exhale in relief.

"What did you do?" her mother demanded, concern fading into exasperation.

"I have two bloodlines," Erin managed to croak out like it explained everything as she pushed herself up. She smiled drunkenly up at her mother. "See, no harm done, and now we're safe here." She held her hand up to her mother. The cut she made had vanished. Instead, there was a thin red line that ran across the plane of her palm that would undoubtedly fade in time, leaving no trace at all.

"Well, next time, warn me when you're about to do complicated pieces of magic," chided her mother. "We could have done it together, and you wouldn't be in this state."

Erin met her mother's eyes, confused. Behind her mother's stern expression, Erin saw terror, the terror of losing a daughter. Erin ducked her head in shame. "Sorry, mom …"

Her mother's face softened. She reached out to tuck a stray strand of hair behind Erin's ear. "It's done and over now," her mother sighed. "I guess we might as well go see the fruits of your work."

Erin's mother grasped her under her arm and hoisted her back to her feet. "You are definitely your father's daughter. If I had a dollar for every crazy venture your father did, I could buy my own island and maybe have a few moments of peace from you two risk takers."

Erin let out a weak chuckle and let her mother steer her towards the front door. When the two women opened the door, Connor was nowhere in sight. Instead, they saw the two valleys huddled down, eyes wide in fright. Erin felt a wave of calm and reassurance flow from her mother down to the two men below. Their eyes glazed over and stood straight.

"Forget what you saw," Erin's mother commanded, her voice filled with power. "Just know that you are safe and everything is all right. Continue on with your duty. By tomorrow morning, it will seem nothing more than a nightmare."

The men slowly nodded before returning to their normal posts. Erin felt another flash of pride over her mother's new-found confidence in using her powers. Not bad for someone who only learned about their ability only a short year ago.

Stumbling back inside, Erin headed to the spot where Connor stood only moments before, picking up the necklace he had dropped in alarm. She traced the etching on the pendant with her finger. She wanted to be angry. She could feel it sputtering to life inside her, but she didn't have enough left in her to fuel it. She turned to face her mother.

"I'm leaving for Louisiana tonight," Erin said, clenching the pendant tight. "I'm going to get Laura back. I …"

The events of the night and the past two days finally caught up to her. She should have known that she couldn't sustain herself with a few stolen hours of sleep and finger food. Her vision went black again, and she crumbled to the floor for the second time. Her mother managed to catch her before she smashed her head on the floor. Erin heard her mother shouting her name, but it sounded far away. The last thing she saw before her world was consumed by darkness was her mother's worried face.

The light hurt her eyes. Erin groaned, pulling the thick comforter over her head. She gasped in pain. Every part of her body hurt. Moaning, she burrowed deeper into her blankets, planning on taking the day off. Fae will just have to get by without her, and there would absolutely be *no* training today. Erin took a deep breath, and her whole body turned to stone. Something was off. Something was wrong. The sheets didn't smell like her sheets. The bed wasn't her bed. The sounds coming from beyond the room were not from her home. She cracked open an eye confirming that she was indeed not in her own bed.

Erin flung the blankets off, leaping to her feet. She ignored her body's protest, blinking rapidly to dispel the stars from her eyes. Her heart thundered in her chest, but no magic answered her call. She was completely tapped out. Slowly, she remembered where she was and why she had come. She looked around her old room, surprised at how little it had changed since she last saw it.

Her eyes took in the soft green walls that she had painted herself during her eighth-grade year. The noonday sun poured in from her large bay window framed by sheer cream-colored curtains. Her eyes were soon drawn to the myriad of photos that took up much of the wall space and tops of her desk and dressers. Painfully, she shuffled over to them; her whole life laid out before her, captured in each frame. She saw childhood toys and friends. She saw parties and good times. The year she got her first bike. Christmas with her family. School plays and graduations. Everything all the way up to when John, her now ex-husband, purposed to her. In the corners of her vanity mirror, she had stuffed concert tickets and dig site photos. Over the corners, she had hung spelling bee medals and Mardi Gras beads.

Looking out over her past, Erin felt a bitter sadness. Sadness at all she had lost, at all she stood left to lose. She wished she wasn't a Guardian. She wished she could go back to when she was ignorant of the magical world and its dangers. *No.* She shook her head. No, she didn't want to go back. Sure, her life had been easier back then, but it wasn't who she truly was meant to be. Danger or not, she had never felt so sure of any path she had ever chosen until now.

The door to her room swung open, revealing her grandmother bearing a silver tray laden with breakfast food and a steaming cup of coffee. Erin's stomach grumbled loudly at the smell of the food, demanding her to eat them right at that very moment or suffer the consequences.

Erin plopped back onto her bed, drooling over the food on the tray. She tore into her meal—bacon, oatmeal, and fresh fruit—not caring that her manners were terrible. Her grandmother chuckled.

"You know, if you ever stop this whole lone wolf role you're so keen on taking, you might become the strongest of us. I don't think I have *ever* seen one of our line come up with such a brilliant idea on the fly like you did last night." Her grandmother chuckled again, shaking her head at the antics of her granddaughter and matriarch.

Erin could only smile sheepishly as she stuffed more food into her mouth. "You would think she was raised by wolves," commented her mother dryly as she walked through the door. Though her words sounded harsh, their effect was somewhat diminished by the laughter in her eyes and the way her mouth curled up at the corners. Erin smiled up at her mother. Her smile fell when she saw her duffle bag in her mother's hand.

"I added a few toiletries for you," her mother said, noting Erin's stare; her smile had become strained. "I also printed out the directions to the work site where your sister was spending her summer at." Her mother bit her lip—much like Erin did when she was upset or had a lot on her mind.

"Thank you."

Her mother and grandmother shared a quick glance before her mother sighed, sitting at the foot of Erin's bed. Her breakfast turned to lead in her stomach.

"There's something that I never got around to telling you last night because of our guest." Her mother's eyes burned bright with anger. She shook her head and continued. "You sister called as often as she could, but she also sent letters."

Erin tilted her head. "Letters?"

Her mother nodded. "She claimed that strange things, accidents and what not, were happening at the work sites. She sent letters because it's easier to hide a paper trail than a digital one. She wanted guidance."

"About what?" Erin asked.

This time, it was her grandmother who answered. "She had a feeling that the accidents that were happening were caused by something supernatural. They happened too frequently. At first, she thought that it might be the work of spirits. There has been a rise in spectral sightings in Louisiana, especially in the bayous, since that hurricane ripped through there."

Erin vaguely remembered hearing about the class five hurricane that destroyed much of the Gulf coast area. "What does that have to do with the accidents?"

"Construction can stir up spirits," her grandmother explained.

"Were her suspicions correct?"

Her grandmother shrugged. "The last message we received from Laura was that she thought that she found someone who might be able to help her. Laura was on her way to see this person when she vanished."

Erin furrowed her brow. "Did you tell this to the police?"

Her mother shook her head. "They wouldn't believe us, and if Laura was right, then we would be sending innocent people to the slaughter."

Erin nodded, agreeing with their reasoning, and sipped her coffee. It had been flavored just the way she liked it. Dutifully, she took a bite of her remaining breakfast. With each bite, she felt more like her old self. As Erin ate, she processed this new piece of information. It wasn't much to go on, but it was a small lead, and given the vision she had, she had no doubt that her sister had been taken by someone with magic. She could feel the weight of the other two women's gaze on her. She knew that they were waiting for her to say something, anything that they could latch onto to give them hope. But she had nothing to offer them, and she hated herself for that.

THREE

THE AIR PRESSED in on Erin like a warm, wet blanket, only a few degrees shy of being oppressive. Walking out of the terminal felt more like entering a new, strange world than a different region in the country of her birth. A thousand new and exotic sights, sounds, and smells assaulted her senses, each one demanding her full and undivided attention. The Deep South could definitely be considered another country, possibly even another world. But Louisiana, more importantly, New Orleans, was something else entirely. Never before had she seen a mix of modernity and antiquity. All around her, locals and tourists alike hustled about jumping in and out of the seemingly never-ending line of taxis. Erin stood just off to the side, attempting to adjust to the sudden change. Each breath she took was heavy on her tongue and coated it with the tiniest hints of spice that the Crescent City was known for. However, it was nearly overpowered by the combined taste-smell of exhaust and sea brine. Over the noise of the terminal around her, Erin could hear jazz music playing somewhere in the distance. It brought a smile to her face.

"First time in New Orleans?"

Startled, Erin jumped, turning towards the source of the voice. The voice belonged to a young-looking cabbie. He couldn't have been more than in his mid-twenties. His skin was so deeply tanned that he could have passed for a difference race if not for the sun bleached hair that curled around his thin face. He flashed Erin a brilliant smile, his rich brown eyes dancing with amusement. His clothing was bright and colorful and loose around his swimmer's frame.

"Sorry, didn't mean to scare you." His accent sounded off. He wasn't a local but had lived there long enough to pick up some of the local speech patterns. "A lot of people get that look when they first see the city."

Erin arched a brow. "What look?"

"The 'Oh my god this place' look." He chuckled kind-heartedly. The corner of Erin's mouth twitched as she fought to keep her expression neutral, but the laughter in her eyes gave her away. The cabbie flashed another bright smile and bowed. "Young Thomas at your service, ma'am."

Erin cocked her head to the side. *"Young* Thomas?"

Young Thomas shrugged. "There's an elderly dude who has the same name. He's been around for a lot longer than anyone can remember, so I end up being 'Young' Thomas."

"I'm sorry to hear that ... I suppose," Erin teased. Young Thomas shrugged again and looked at her expectantly. "Unfortunately, I'm not staying in the city. I'm actually heading further south towards the bayous. I just need to pick up my car."

Young Thomas laughed. "Yeah, that would be a hell of a fare. No worries. If you find your way back this way and find yourself in need of a ride slash guide, give me a holler." He presented Erin with a business card with all the flourish of a street magician. Erin laughed as she took it.

She bid Young Thomas a hearty farewell before following the signs to the rental car lots.

"If you think this place is strange," Young Thomas called after her, "just wait 'til you meet them bayou boys!"

Erin laughed and waved goodbye without looking back.

The car she got from the rental place was small but comfortable enough. It wasn't like she needed that much space. No, the car had been chosen more for its gas economy than its size. The further from the city she got, the more her worries began to eat at her calm. They slowly took over her mind until the outside world ceased to exist for her. She didn't see the sprawling plantations or the tree laden with Spanish moss. She didn't even see the road ahead of her. Her mind had retreated, leaving her body to act purely out on autopilot. What she did see was every dark possibility she could face once she reached the sight of her sister's disappearance.

Little towns popped up and went by. Soon, the only thing that surrounded Erin's little car was vast emptiness of marshy lands. Finally, she pulled off the lonely highway to stop. The sign above the little truck stop read *Last Stop Station.*

The truck stop wasn't much; just a rundown building where the outside plaster was slowly flaking away. One of the letters on the sign flickered, threatening to die at any given moment. The parking lot was nothing more than a gravel lot. The pumps looked like they should have been put into a museum fifty years ago. Either way, she pulled up next to them and got out of her car with a groan. She placed her hands on her lower back and arched backward. A sigh escaped her lips as her spine popped, releasing the pressure that had been steadily building for the past five miles.

A paper sign on the pump stated that all gas purchases had to be made inside first. With an indifferent huff, Erin walked towards the crumbling building, taking long strides to stretch out her stiff legs.

The inside wasn't much better than the outside. Her nose crinkled at the aroma of stale cigarettes and beer. It looked like no one had bothered to clean the place in god knows how long. That didn't bode well for the restroom she needed to use.

The clerk hadn't bothered to look up when Erin entered. She was more interested in her phone, her fingers rapidly dancing across its screen. Her dark hair hung lank about her ashen face. Her cheeks were scared and pitted.

Black eyeliner did nothing to hide the deadness of her pale eyes. Her thin lips were pressed tightly together, making the lines around them stand out even more. Every so often she would suck her teeth, sneering at whatever held her attention. Her tank top boasted a number of old faded stains and was so stretched out that it barely covered her black sports bra. She looked rough and gave off the aura that she could explode at any given moment. Erin cautiously saddled up next to the counter. She waited for the clerk to acknowledge her, but she didn't.

"Twenty dollars of regular on pump one," she said, slamming a bill on the counter. The clerk rolled her eyes, took the money and entered in the purchase. "Gotta bathroom?"

Another sigh. The clerk dug out a dingy little key attached to a blackened piece of wood.

Erin cringed, using only two fingers to pick it up. As she walked towards the back where the disease-ridden restroom most likely was, she heard the clerk mutter "Uppity bitch."

Green-gold light flashed briefly in Erin's eyes as she spun around. The few working lights flickered out. The sparsely stocked shelves quivered. The clerk didn't seem to notice anything strange until her phone flew out of her hands, hitting the floor with a satisfying clatter. Even from her position near the back, Erin could see that the screen had cracked. A small smirk graced her face as she turned her back on the cursing clerk.

The restroom wasn't as bad as she had thought, surprisingly. It was still on the dirty side but didn't make her want to get a hazmat suit. Guilt caught up to her as she washed her hands in the rust-stained sink. She had let her frayed nerves get the better of her when she lashed out. She was better than that. To make up for her tantrum, Erin bought snacks that she didn't need. As if that would make up for her breaking something that probably had cost the clerk a couple of paychecks.

"So why is this place called *Last Stop*?" Erin asked as she set her items down.

The clerk popped her gum. "Prolly because dis is da last station before Moonbay Bayou. No utter station til dere."

Erin nodded her head in faked interest, paid for the junk food, then went on to top off her tank. As she waited for the pump to stop, her mind wandered to her task, to what brought her to this muggy portion of the world. Per her navigational system, she had another several hours of driving until she arrived at her destination—Moonbay Bayou. She had no idea what to expect when she got there or what type of reception she would receive. She figured the local police wouldn't be happy to have her around, snooping on her own and harassing them. But she was more curious about how the magical community would react to her. She knew nothing about bayou magic or voodoo. She didn't want to make enemies while attempting to rescue her sister.

Performing her own investigation would be a tricky thing. Erin would have to be extra careful not to attract any unwanted attention from the local police or from the person or persons responsible for her sister's disappearance. The same people who took Laura could very well be on the lookout for her.

Erin pursed her lips. She would *never* be someone's prey again.

In the back seat of her car sat her trusty duffle bag, the very same one she used to flee her abusive ex. Erin opened it and pulled out a stack of letters, surprisingly thick; each and every one written by her sister. Who knew Laura was such a letter writer? Erin smiled until she read the first letter.

The date on the letter was months before Laura disappeared and had been written while she had been in school.

I had another close call a few days ago. I was meditating, trying to go to astral plane, I'm still struggling on my own, and apparently I caused fog to form in my room. Luckily I was able to convince my roommate that I was messing with dry ice. I don't think she really believes me though.

I feel bad hiding this part of me from my friends, but I don't think they could really handle the truth. You know? Plus, some are like uber *conservative. I'm worried if they find out the truth about me, they won't want anything to do with me. I don't think I could handle them turning on me.*

Erin frowned into the letter. She understood precisely how her sister felt, and it hurt that she hadn't reached out to her. They had always been close, shared everything. Perhaps Laura felt that Erin was simply too far away to offer any help. Either way, it hurt.

She reached for another letter. It was more pleasant. She could almost feel her sister's excitement through the letter as she described Moonbay. The letter also bore the telltale signs of magic scorching brought about by strong emotions. Erin read the letter in its entirety twice over, scanning for every bit of information she could.

Moonbay Bayou was more than just an area of swampy land; it was also a small fishing town that bore the same name. Erin figured that the founders either wanted to keep things simple or lacked imagination. It sounded much like every small town across the country and around the world. The locals were nice but mostly kept to themselves. The food was out of this world. Erin felt another twinge of guilt when she read just how excited Laura was over the magical community there. Her sister was slightly surprised at how strong it was but was over the moon to finally have someone to talk to about magic. Apparently, her sister no longer felt like she could confide in her big sister—and why should she?

As soon as Erin accepted her role, her mother, grandmother, and sister went back to their home, and she hadn't given them a passing thought since. Sure, she called her grandmother from time to time, but only when she needed something from her. She never asked how her mother's or sister's training was going. Nor had she offered to help. Not even when she discovered a long lost magical library that held centuries of knowledge with a magic-boosting sigil carved into the floor that helped new witches practice the spells essential for their survival. Her stomach turned sour. No wonder her sister had become prey to some backwater dark practitioner. Erin had done nothing, *nothing*, to ensure to the safety of her family. She had just taken the bulk of her family's power and run with it. With a heavy heart, she read another letter.

It became evident that Laura had fallen in love with the charms of Moonbay bayou and its people. In several of her letters, she talked about returning to the town after she was done with college and opening a small boutique where the clothing was inspired by the wild beauty around the sleepy little town. Erin could almost see the shop in her mind, but the image was blurry, almost as if it was held under murky water. If she didn't save Laura, then it wouldn't matter what her dreams had been; they would never come to be.

Erin gently tucked the letters back into the duffle bag. They, plus the necklace she reclaimed from Conner, were her only links to Laura. She hoped to use them to find her sister. Filled with a renewed sense of purpose, Erin got back on the road and headed towards Moonbay Bayou. She would find out its true nature for herself soon enough.

The sun was nothing more than half a golden ball of light along the horizon when Erin finally reached the town of Moonbay Bayou. The early evening sky was a riot of colors she never thought possible—rich purples, bloody reds, glittery golds, the softest of pinks, and the palest of blues. The waters that surrounded the sleepy-looking town mirrored back the colors, making blurring the lines between water and sky. It was as if, out there on the water, there was no beginning or end; everything just ... was.

Erin drove through the quiet streets and couldn't help but draw similarities to Dorshire. Both places had the feel of being partially stuck in the past, with the old buildings still bearing the faded names of businesses long gone painted onto the sides. The people were friendly, smiling at one another when they passed in the streets. Time seemed to slow, and the frantic energy that simmered in Erin's veins eased to a dull hum. But it was there that the similarities ended. Whereas Dorshire buildings were simple and plain, every building in Moonbay was a different color. There were some that bore more traditional coloring with their whitewashed exterior trimmed with dark woods. But most were painted in such a multitude of vibrant colors that Erin couldn't help but think about Mardi Gras. But even with all the differences in the décor and color schemes, there was not a single building that did not fit.

Dozens of ships were moored along the weathered docks. Where the buildings were a riot of colors, the ships were plain and practical. These were the boats of the working fisherman. A couple of boats were still out, gliding across the picturesque water, leaving multicolored waves in their wake.

No wonder Laura had fallen in love with the sleepy little town.

Erin got out of her car with a groan. Her back was on fire and about as stiff as a board. Exhaustion burned around the edges of her eye, and the one thing she desired at that moment was a hot bath and a soft bed. And while nothing would make her happier than to take some time to relax and recharge, she had more important things to attend to.

The hotel where she booked her room was called *Crescent Days*. A bronze placard near the front door informed her that the hotel had been one of the first buildings ever built in the town, and while it had changed names and ownerships over the years, it had always been an inn. Erin smiled. Old but taken care of; just the way she liked it.

The inside was cozy but immaculate. Nothing appeared out of place, and yet it still had that lived-in feel to it. After checking in and getting her key—a real key, not a keycard—Erin trudged up to her room. It was more of a suite actually. She didn't know exactly how long she would have to stay in Moonbay, and she wanted to be somewhat comfortable. She also needed the space to prepare her spells and charms for when she found her sister. It was pricey but a necessary cost and one that she would gladly make a thousand times over if that is what would bring her sister safely home again.

It was a nice suite, although it felt more like a studio apartment than a hotel suite. Erin walked into her temporary home with the same happiness she felt walking into her own home. Her eyes were instantly drawn to the plush queen-sized bed just off to the left of the living space.

Her bags were dropped unceremoniously to the floor as her feet mindlessly carried her to the bed. She stepped around the love seat, completely ignoring the kitchenette to her right, throwing herself face-first into the mound of pillows at the head of the bed. The mattress was thick and squishy. She sighed with contentment as her aching and exhausted body sunk into it, but she couldn't enjoy it for long.

Erin rolled herself off the bed, even though every part of her body cried out against it. If she lay there a second longer, she would have succumbed to sleep. She still had an hour, maybe two, of useable daylight left, and she planned to use every last second of it.

As she unpacked, a tingling sensation crept over her skin. At first, she didn't really pay the sensation much mind—she had been traveling almost non-stop for nearly a week—but then she saw small flashes of light from the corners of her eyes. Erin rubbed her burning eyes. Perhaps she should take a small nap if she was hallucinating. But as she thought about it, there was something oddly familiar about the tingling and the flashes of light. Her tired brain finally registered what she was experiencing—magic! It was not the magic that came from a practitioner. This was the magic of the land. But it wasn't like anything she had ever felt before. She wished Fae had been able to join her. She missed his insight and the reassurance his presence gave her. It made sense to leave him back home, but she wondered what he would have made of all the magic simmering in the air.

After grabbing one of her remaining energy drinks, Erin headed off to her first stop of the night—the police station. Better to get that out of the way first.

The police station was a hub of activity, with phones ringing ever few breaths being answered by haggard-looking officers. Erin raised a brow, pausing only for a moment before cautiously stepping up to the front desk where the dispatch officer bounced between two calls.

"Car two-five-six, the dispute is at fifty-eight Moss Lane."

The officer's voice on the other end crackled through the handheld radio. "Affirmative. On the way, car two-five-six clear."

The dispatcher hung up one phone and turned his attention to the other. "Sorry about that, ma'am. Could you repeat that?" He grabbed a pencil and wrote down on a pad of paper. "I understand, ma'am, but as long as the dog stays on its owner's property, we can't do anything about its barking. Dogs bark." The caller said something else—or shouted it rather.

Erin could hear the angry tone from where she stood. The dispatcher closed his eyes and released a heavy sigh. "Ma'am, you're just going to have to either live with it or try to work it out with your neighbor. Good-day."

The dispatcher hung up the phone with just a little more force than necessary. It was then that he noticed Erin standing in front of him. He didn't even bother to put on a fake smile. His weary eyes bored into hers as he grumbled: "What can I do for you?"

Erin fought the urge to shrink under his irritated gaze. "Um ... I am Erin McManin, Laura Ripley's older sister."

The dispatcher looked at her blandly.

"You know, the missing college student," Erin elaborated, surprised and a little alarmed until she saw a light of recognition in the dispatcher's eyes.

"Yes, the missing student. We've told your family everything we got." His eyes narrowed, confused as to why Erin stood before him.

"I understand, but all the same, I'm here until my sister is found. Is there someone in charge of her case that I can talk to?"

The dispatcher let out an exasperated sigh, leaning back in his chair. "Detective Remy Mercier. He's in the third office on the right." He waved Erin through and went back to answering the main line that was already ringing. "Must be a full moon," the dispatcher muttered, exasperated.

No one stopped Erin or even looked her way as she walked deeper into the bowels of the police station, looking for the name the dispatcher had given her. She spotted it finally on one of the frosted glass doors near the very back of the building. The door was closed, but she could hear a muffled voice deep and steady on the other side. She gave the door a few short raps. The voice on the other side of the door faltered. Erin heard the confident stride that created the image of an older, but still in his prime, detective whose hair had only just begun to gray. The man who opened the door was not that at all.

Erin took a step back. "I'm looking for Detective Mercier."

The man in front of her couldn't have been much older than Erin. She couldn't narrow his age down because of the mop of red curls on top of his head. They gave him a more youthful appearance. His clothing made him look more like a man you'd pass on the street rather than a detective. His jeans were slightly worn and frayed around the hems. His boots were heavily scuffed. The only thing semi-professional he wore was a dark green button-up shirt, although the sleeves had been rolled up to his elbows and the shirt was wrinkled as if he had slept in it.

The young man flashed Erin a cocky smile and looked her up and down, wary intrigued in his warm brown eyes. "Well, now, what can I do for you, chér?"

"Are you Detective Remy Mercier?"

The detective smiled a little brighter. "That I am. And you are?"

"Laura Renly's sister. Erin McManin."

Detective Mercier's carefree smile faded. He studied Erin again—this time, marking the similarities she shared with her sister. He stepped aside and ushered her into his office.

The office was sparsely furnished. A large desk covered in paperwork took up most of the available space. The only other furnishings were a couple of chairs and a tall bookcase filled with reference materials. A small leafy plant clung to life hanging limply to one side of the bookcase. Only one wall held any adornments—a complex-looking map with her sister's picture in the middle.

Erin felt drawn to the smiling face of her sister. A small part wondered if she would ever see that smile again. She closed her eyes and turned away from the wall, swallowing down the tide of her emotions. When she opened her eyes, she saw the detective watching her closely.

"I'm sorry that you and your family are going through this," he said, taking a seat at his desk.

Erin's throat tightened as she took a seat in the other chair. "Thank you."

"Do you have any new information that you need to share?"

Erin shook her head. "I don't live in the country," she explained. "I came back as soon as I heard. I'm here to help you find my sister."

Detective Mercier leaned forward onto his elbows. "Miss McManin ..."

"Erin please, detective."

"Then call me Remy," he said, flashing another charming smile before becoming serious once again. "We already have dozens of capable and highly trained officers already on your sister's case. Now unless you're an officer too, wherever you're from ..." Erin shook her head. "Then I'm afraid you'll only be in the way."

Erin bristled at his words. "I'm sure you have your best men on it, but I highly doubt college students will be as open to your *officers* as they would be with me."

"Perhaps, but they are *quite open* with me."

Erin understood what he meant. In any other case, the detective's youthful appearance would have been a hindrance. But when dealing with younger witnesses, he could make himself appear to be no different than them. Erin leaned back in her chair, chewing on her lip. But still, a cop was a cop. She would seek them out herself, no matter what the detective said.

She slumped back into her seat, the perfect picture of resignation. "Has there been any developments?"

Remy shook his head, leaning on his elbows. "Unfortunately no; all we have is what we told your parents. Your sister was a part of a volunteer group that was helping to rebuild some of the fishing cabins and homes that had been destroyed by that big hurricane a while back. Moonbay has always depended on tourism for much of its income. Our bayous are one of the best, and the same goes for our fishing industry, both commercial and private. Katrina hit us hard, just like everywhere else.

"Anyway, things were going well at the construction sites, but about two weeks before your sister's disappearance, accidents started to happen. We think that the accidents and your sister's disappearance are connected."

A chill ran down Erin's spine. "You do?" she asked, breathless.

Remy nodded. "The less scrupulous members of our population took advantage of all the abandoned fishing huts and homes along the bayous. And they aren't too happy about people coming around and fixing these places up."

"You have suspects?"

Remy smirked at her. "You know I can't tell you that."

Erin's lower extremities coiled tightly in reaction to the detective's smirk that promised all sorts of fun to be if only she had the courage to take part in them. Startled, she stood up and reached into her purse. "Thought I give it a try," she said with forced composure. She pulled out a small business card. "This is where I'm staying. You can reach me there if there are any developments. I'm not leaving until my sister is found."

Remy took the card and watched as Erin walked quickly towards the door. "I'll find your sister," he said just as she reached out for the doorknob.

There was something in his voice that urged Erin to look over her shoulder. Detective Remy leaned back in his chair, his face utterly serious. His promise charged the space between them, but the moment faded as the mischievous light returned to Remy's eyes. "And when I do, we can go out for drinks and celebrate."

Erin laughed in spite of herself and rolled her eyes as she walked out. Playboy or not, Detective Remy was her best shot at finding Laura. She had no doubt that he would find Laura, one way or another.

Back in her rental car, Erin hit the road again. She had one more stop to make before she could call it a day.

The areas where they were rebuilding were deep within the bayous, only accessible by boat, but the campsite where most of the volunteers were staying was on the outskirts of town. It wouldn't be too long a ride.

Camper and tents filled up nearly every last inch of available space. Erin had to park her car right at the entrance to the camp. Most of the people milling about looked to be college students, but there were a few adults present in a chaperone capacity. Erin made a beeline for one of the older residents of the campsite. Once she explained who she was, they directed her towards the camper Laura shared with a few of her friends before she disappeared.

A pop song that Erin didn't recognize blasted from the speakers of an old radio outside the camper that she had been directed to. The camper had seen better days. Much of the exterior was covered in rust. It was hard for Erin to believe that the rickety, rusted bucket in front of her had been her sister's home away from home before her disappearance. The windows were dark, and despite the music, the camper appeared to have been empty. Erin cautiously placed her foot on a wobbly cinder block and rapped on the door. Her knock was answered by a blurry eyed girl with a messy, pink, pixie cut.

"Whad ja want?" the girl yawned, glaring at Erin.

"Are you Rebecca?"

"Yeah," the girl drawled, leaning up against the door frame. Erin could feel the girl's apprehension and suspicion.

"I'm Laura's sister, Erin. I was wondering if I could talk to you or one of her other friends about her disappearance."

"We already told the cops everything," Rebecca snipped, instantly going on the defensive. "I had nothing to do with it, and I don't know any."

"Hey, I'm not here to lay blame," Erin said calmly, holding her hands out in a non-threatening manner. "I appreciate all the help you've given the cops, but I was wondering if there was anything that you didn't tell them. Something that you thought they might not believe or that might make Laura look bad?"

The young woman bit her lip. Erin could almost see the internal conflict raging inside Rebecca's mind. Erin didn't press, didn't try to take advantage of Rebecca's indecision. She didn't want Laura's friend to shut her out completely. So, Erin held her breath until her sister's friend motioned for her to enter the camper. Her knees quivered in relief.

The inside of the camper was a wreck. Clothes and empty food containers were everywhere. Rebecca started to clean up. Erin waited a few moments for the girl to speak, but it soon became clear that she was going to have to get the conversation started.

"How well did you actually know my sister?" Erin asked; a simple enough question to get the conversation started.

Rebecca leaned up against the counter, fiddling with a soda bottle. "Well enough, I guess. We bunked in the same hall, had a couple of classes together and ran with the same crowds. I wouldn't say that we were like best friends or anything, but still friends. She was … is a great person, always willing to lend a hand even if she …"

"Even if she what?" Erin pressed.

"Nothing," Rebecca muttered. She turned and continued with her cleaning. Erin knew what the girl was doing; Erin used to do the same thing when asked uncomfortable questions. By keeping her hands and body moving, Rebecca hoped to keep her secrets to herself. Urgency flooded Erin's body. There was no time to beat about the bush. Erin needed to show her hand and hope that everything turned out for the best.

"You know there's something *different* about my sister, don't you?"

Rebecca slowly turned around and met Erin's gaze. Neither one of the women blinked until the younger woman's shoulders slumped. "I guess you would know better than anyone." She hopped up onto the counter. Erin was slightly surprised that Rebecca hadn't fallen through.

"Strange things always seem to happen around Laura. Our dorm would always get these power surges or outages whenever she was upset or really stressed out." Rebecca glanced at Erin sidelong. Erin smiled and urged her to continue. "There were a lot of other things too, but that's not really important. When we got here, Laura instantly fell in love with this place. She said that the land welcomed her or something like that."

Erin swallowed the lump in her throat. Meanwhile, Rebecca continued on, unable to stop now that the floodgates had been opened.

"Not long after we started fixing up the homes, things started to go all wrong. Machines wouldn't work. Supplies went missing, and some people got hurt; one really bad. A few of the others joked that it was a haunting, but …"

"Laura didn't think so," Erin finished. Rebecca nodded.

"She found this local voodoo lady—can you believe that—and was going to see her. I don't know if she did or not, but a few days later, she was gone. No note. No calls. Nothing." Rebecca wrapped her arms around her thin frame.

"Do you have a name?"

"No, but Laura made friends with a local ... Jacque, I think. Works as a mechanic in town. I never met him, but I heard Laura talk about him all the time. He might be able to tell you."

Erin stood, her whole body buzzing with a renewed sense of vigor. "Thanks for your help."

"Just find her," Rebecca pleaded. "Laura's one of the best people I know. I wouldn't be here right now if it wasn't for her. Please just find her."

Erin pulled the younger woman in for a tight embrace before returning to her car. Rebecca's tiny frame quivered with fear and sorrow. Erin made some comforting sounds, rubbing circles on the girl's back until she calmed down. Erin gave her one last embrace before walking out into the fading light. It was too late for Erin to pursue this lead. As much as she hated to, she would have to wait until morning. Any garages would most likely be closed by the time she made it back to town. Even though she was frustrated about having to wait, a small glimmer of hope blossomed inside. The trail wasn't cold, at least not for her. The police may not have any new leads, but they were looking at the situation from the wrong angle.

A quick internet search back in her suite gave her several garages in town that she would have to visit one by one until she located Jacque. Not a pleasant prospect. She entered them in on her phone for the morning. She ordered takeout for dinner, too drained from the day to deal with anything else. She showered and called her mother to fill her in. They talked until her food arrived—fried catfish with hush puppies and collard greens. She ate without tasting any of it. For all she cared, she ate the air itself. The only way she knew that she actually ate food instead of hallucinating it was the heavy feeling in her stomach. She had one last call to make before she finally gave in to what her body was incessantly demanding.

"Orrin."

"Hey," Erin croaked.

"Erin! What have you found out? Are you OK? Things are fine here, just so you know."

Erin smiled weakly. "Nothing really new, but I do have a lead. The nature magic here is a little odd, though."

"Not surprising," commented Orrin.

"Oh? Do tell."

"The area's swampy, right? Well, that makes it an in-between place, not quite land but not quite water. In-between places have different energies than other places. Some would even say more powerful."

"Huh, interesting," Erin mused. "Thanks for that and for holding down the fort while I'm off playing detective. I really appreciate it."

"Hey, no problem. What are friends for?"

Erin laughed into the phone. "Well, I need to hit the hay. I'll call you if anything exciting happens."

"Happy hunting," Orrin joked. "I hope you find Laura all right. Do you want me to see if my brother can divine anything?"

"Oh Orrin, no. I appreciate the offer but no. Your brother suffers enough. Laura and I have a connection. I'll give that a tug."

Orrin heaved a sigh of relief on the other end. Erin wasn't sure if he meant to or not. "I'll let you go. Sleep tight."

"And don't let the bedbugs bite," Erin finished. She hung up the phone and settled down into her bed with a heavy sigh, her body sinking into the warm and soft mattress.

But even with being tired right down to her bones, sleep eluded Erin. She spent half the night tossing and turning in the unfamiliar bed, missing her usual bed partner Fae, and the other half she spent being tormented by visions of her sister bound and gagged, surrounded by menacing figures.

Erin's list bore one scratch mark after another. With each stop, each black line drawn, her spirit sank further into the pits of despair. Erin pulled up to a small, dingy-looking garage. It was the last one on her list. If Jacque didn't work at the *Manic Mechanics,* then the trail would be cold for her. She had no other leads to go on other than the voodoo woman her sister reached out to. But that one was even shakier than finding a mechanic named Jacque. The bayou towns were littered with hundreds, if not thousands, of voodoo practitioners. Who knew if the one her sister found even lived in Moonbay? She also doubted that the police would divulge any unmetered information to her. Erin shook her head. If Jacque wasn't here, she would have to resort to more drastic—magical—measures.

The scents of gas, motor oil, and cigarettes tinged with greasy food assaulted her senses as soon as she exited her vehicle. It was the exact same smell at each of the other garages she visited that day. What was it about garages that caused them to all have the same disgusting aromas? The motor oil and gas made sense, but cigarettes and fast food? She shook her head.

Through one of the open bay doors, Erin spied a car that could have come straight out of a seventies' movie. A mechanic was halfway into the engine bay. Erin heard the unmistakable sound of a ratchet turning as she got closer. From the depths of the open hood, the mechanic quietly cursed at whatever was giving him trouble. Erin cleared her throat as she approached, as to not startle the mechanic, causing him to hit his head or drop his tool.

"Be with you in a sec," the mechanic replied, startling Erin. It was a woman's voice that came from the depths of the vehicle.

"Uh, no rush, I was wondering if someone called Jacque worked here. I need to ask him a few questions about the girl who disappeared."

The mechanic visibly stiffened and slowly straightened back up, bringing Erin face to face with a young African America woman with almond colored skin, vibrant amber eyes, and thick, onyx dreadlocks twisted up into a bun. Her baggy, grease-stained overalls added bulk to her spindly frame body that it couldn't provide on its own.

"I'm Jacque," she said as she scrutinized Erin. "I already told the police everything that I know. I don't have time to talk to reporters too."

Erin blanched. "I'm not a reporter. I'm her sister, Erin."

Jacque's amber eyes showed no emotion as she continued to glare at Erin with guarded suspicion. "Please," Erin begged. Jacque sighed, looking towards the heavens before heading to the waiting room. Erin remained where she stood, unsure until the other woman beckoned her with a jerk of her chin.

The office area was just as filthy as the rest of the garage and smelling stronger of greasy fast food. Once inside, Jacque let down her dreads, letting them cascade down her back like rivers of velvety night. Bits of silver flashed in the dim light like stars in the sky, the only bit of jewelry Erin could see on the mechanic. Jacque then poured a cup of coffee so black—it might as well have been tar—and handed it to Erin.

"My full name's Jacqueline Déco. Sorry 'bout the grease on the cup, but there's no escaping it 'round here."

"That's all right," Erin replied, quickly taking the cup, but she didn't take a sip. One, it was too hot for coffee, and two, she was more interested in what the young mechanic had to say.

"I liked your sister," Jacque admitted, leaning up against the door frame to the garage. "She was real nice, smiled at everyone, and didn't judge. It's hard to find that quality in people these days. I'm sorry she's missing, and I hope they find her soon, but I don't think I can help ya."

This time, it was Erin's turn to scrutinize; everything about Jacque's body language screamed secret. Whatever she knew, she didn't want the police or Erin to know about it. But this was her sister's life. She didn't have the time or the patience to worry about someone else's baggage, not with the visions she's been having.

Erin took a shot in the dark. "Then why did my sister come to you about finding a voodoo practitioner?"

Jacque stilled, and Erin knew that her assumptions had been correct. She figured Jacque was the one who turned her sister onto the voodoo priestess. Erin suppressed her smile and watched Jacque, who seemingly had turned to stone. Erin wasn't even sure that she was still breathing.

When Jacque spoke again, her voice was as hard as a tempered steel and carried a lethal edge. "I have no idea what you are talking about. I think it's time for you to go."

Erin did no such thing. She placed the cup with the too strong coffee on the seat beside her and stood straight-backed and met the other woman's gaze head-on. It helped that Jacque was a few inches shorter than Erin. She used that advantage in height to loom over the other woman, trying to appear imposing and moderately threatening. Jacque knew exactly what her sister had been searching for, and Erin was not going to leave without that information. She reached deep inside to the place where her magic dwelled and flung it out into the tiny office. The doors slammed shut and locked themselves. Jacque leaped to the middle of the room, lowering into a fighting stance. Her eyes were wide with alarm, looking at Erin like she was a monster from a fairy tale. Erin pushed her guilt down. The longer her sister remained missing, the less likely it was that she would be found alive. The blinds closed next, throwing the room into a blackness far darker than it had any right to be.

In the darkness, Erin heard Jacques ragged breathing and felt her growing fear, time for Erin to switch tactics. From her palm, a soft green—the color of leaves in spring—pushed back the darkness. In the light, she found Jacque pressed up against the wall on the opposite side of the room. Her skin had taken on an ashy completion, with sweat glistening across her brow.

"Don't assume anything about me or what I am willing to do to save my sister," Erin said in a cold, chipped voice. "I know my sister came to you searching for answers. I know you told her about a person who could give her those answers. You will do the same for me or risk my ire." This was the first time that Erin ever used her abilities as a threat against an innocent person. It left a sour taste in her mouth. A small corner of her mind wondered if Connor ever felt the same as she did in the beginning. What choices, what concessions did he make along his journey? His family couldn't have always been dark. He couldn't have always been dark. If Erin wasn't careful, she knew that she could very well end up being just like him.

Jacque swallowed and closed her eyes. "Come back at six. I'll arrange the meeting."

"Why don't we leave right now?"

"Because you don't just pop in on this person unless you have a death wish." She shot Erin a nasty look. "Those are my terms. Agreed?"

Erin closed her palm with a triumphant smile, and everything returned to normal. "Agreed." She turned to leave but paused at the doorway. She glanced over her shoulder to see Jacque with her hands on her knees, gasping for air. The sweetness of victory turned ash. Guilt tore at Erin's stomach. "I'm sorry," she muttered before walking out and closing the door gently behind her.

FOUR

THE BREEZE THAT came off the bay caressed Erin's skin, gently cooling her as she sat outside a small café just a short walk from her hotel. She had stumbled across the café entirely by accident. After her less than pleasant visit to Jacque's shop, Erin couldn't bear the thought of returning to her room to wait out the day. It still didn't sit right with her how easy it was for her to use her magic as a scare tactic; just how close she was to walking the dark path and becoming the very thing her family swore to defeat. Erin hoped that a walk around town would help to clear her head and give her a better feel for the people. After her breakfast, she planned on spending the rest of the morning and perhaps most of the afternoon visiting the shops. Who knew, perhaps she might be able to pick up on something that could help her save her sister and maybe herself as well.

Erin took another bite of her breakfast—a delicious blueberry scone, with lemon icing drizzled over top. She sighed in pleasure as the buttery texture of the scone rolled over her tongue, blending beautifully with the sweetness of the blueberries and the tartness from the lemon icing. The bitterness of her coffee helped to balance out the sweetness of the scone. Erin reclined back into the iron wroth chair and gazed out onto the bustle streets. Once again, she could understand why her sister had started to fall in love with this sleepy little bayou town. On the surface, everything appeared sleepy and slow, beckoning one to take things slow for once, but if you delved a little deeper; there was this steady outpour of energy that made it nearly impossible to remain still for too long. It was an interesting combination. Erin wondered if all in-between places felt like this.

It was that perplexing combination that urged Erin to her feet right as she downed the last dregs of her coffee. She left the protective shade of the café's awning, threw her trash into the nearest receptacle and let her feet carry her where they willed. She opened herself up to the energies of this seemingly sleepy town, and let them carry her where they willed.

Perhaps unsurprisingly, Erin found her way to what could be nothing else but a store for those who practiced voodoo. The doors to the shop had been left open, giving passersby a tantalizing glimpse inside. Erin peered into the shadowy depths of the shop and felt its pull. She shrugged. What could it hurt to go inside? If this was the style of magic that the locals used, learning something about it could come in handy.

Thousands of artifacts hung from the rafters, brushing the top of Erin's head. She tried to not shutter when it happened. Shelves and display cases were packed to near bursting capacity with candles, incense, feathers, books, and bones. Erin's heart fluttered like a bird caught in a trap as she stared at the bones. She had a sneaking suspicion that some of them were human.

"What can I do you for today?" asked an ethereal voice from somewhere near the back of the shop. Erin squinted into the shadows but couldn't see the speaker.

"I'm a ... just browsing," sputtered Erin. She could feel the other person's amusement over her awkwardness.

"Ya sure, darlin'?" the voice asked, sounding louder. From the back of the shop, a slightly plump, middle-aged woman with skin the color of mahogany came forward. Her ebony hair was only slightly streaked with gray and little bits of stone and feathers had been braided into it. She gave Erin a coy and knowing smile as she gracefully weaved her way through the tight spaces between the shelves.

"I can see a dark shadow hangin' over ya head. I could make it go away."

Sharp pinpricks of pain racked through Erin's mind. She quickly threw up her magic, protecting herself from the other woman's magical probes. The other woman jerked back, startled.

"My apologies," she sputtered, thrusting her hands out in a placating manner.

"It's all right," Erin assured the other woman. "But for future references, you probably shouldn't dig into someone's mind before you know if they're a magic wielder or not." The other woman didn't relax. She took a couple of tentative steps backward, putting more space in between her and Erin. This stung Erin largely because of her early activities. She tried once again to placate the woman.

"My name's Erin. What's yours?"

"You're here because of that girl who's gone missin'," the other woman stammered, reaching up to clutch something around her neck.

Erin nodded. "Yes, my sister Laura. Did she ever come into here?"

The other woman nodded. "All dem kids did. I knew what ya sista was when she walked in me store. She wasn't as good at hidin' it as you." Erin made a noncommittal gesture and let her magic roll off of her like waves to the shore. The other woman closed her eyes as Erin's power washed over her. The worry lines in her face smoothed, and the tension leaked from her body. When she opened her eyes again, she was still wary of Erin, but she no longer feared her.

"My name's Charlotte."

Erin's mouth curved slightly. "Nice to meet you, Charlotte. Can you explain what all this stuff is for?" She gestured to the shop, earning a smile from Charlotte at last. She invited Erin to the back where they shared a drink and gave her a crash course in voodoo.

Several hours later, Erin left the shop with her head reeling. She still didn't have an inkling at what voodoo was exactly, but Charlotte did bestow one kernel of knowledge upon her. After listing the numerous spells, charms, and curses she had performed over the years, Erin had asked her if she ever feared being consumed by the dark for the things she did.

Charlotte chortled, waving her hand at Erin. "You white witches know nothing. Da world isn't split into light an' dark. It's gray. It's a bit of both. Dat's *true* balance, not this mess ya got in ya head."

Erin sat back, chewing on the words. They made sense, *and* they eased the guilt she felt from frightening Jacque. No person in the world, magical or mortal, was solely good or evil—light or dark. Erin felt a pressure lift from her shoulders.

"See, I told ja I could get rid of dat dark cloud," Charlotte beamed.

Erin rolled her eyes and bid the other woman a good day.

"Just come back and see me if ya need anyting else, darlin'!" Charlotte shouted, to which Erin gave an absentminded wave.

As she left the voodoo shop, Erin's stomach growled loudly. She pressed her hand against her stomach, startled. Had breakfast really been that long ago? A quick glance at the sky confirmed what her stomach told her. It was past noon. With a mental shrug and a tiny huff, she went off in search for lunch.

With her nose to the air like a bloodhound, Erin snorted through the multitude of scents in the air. As always, there was the salty brine that wafted up from the waters. That aroma also carried the faintest hints of fish from the day's catch. She detected the mouth-watering, sugary scent of pastries next. And while that would definitely be tasty, it wouldn't fill her belly for long. Erin took another deep breath.

"There you are." Erin had no idea what the tantalizingly spicy aroma came from, but she knew beyond a shadow of a doubt that she wanted it in her belly. Using her nose as a guide, Erin once again wandered the streets of Moonbay. She found the source of the aroma down a small restaurant down a narrow back alley.

The restaurant had no name, or not where Erin could see it. But the wooden sign in the shape of a bowl was enough of a confirmation for her. She pushed through the paint speckled door and into the darkness inside.

The delicate aroma that had led Erin to the inconspicuous restaurant bombarded her nasal passages, causing a tickle in the back of her throat. Her mouth watered the same time her stomach let out a growl that she was sure could be heard all the way back in Dorshire. Plastering a Cheshire smile on her face, Erin made a beeline for the nearest available seat, which coincidentally happened to be right next to the bar. A friendly waitress took her order and in no time at all returned, bearing a delicious tray intended to quell her ravenous stomach. The first forkful was pure heaven. Erin's eye fluttered in delight that only grew with each bite. Bite after bite went down her gullet until there was nothing left but a bit of juice that she eagerly sopped up with a bit of bread. Full to the point of being stuffed, she leaned back, rubbing her hands over her slightly expanded stomach. The weight of her meal settled heavily in her stomach, making her feel warm and sleepy. A large yawn erupted from her mouth. A small nap wouldn't hurt. She still had several hours before she needed to head over to see Jacque. It might actually be in her best interest to get a little bit of sleep before her meeting.

Erin paid her bill, leaving a hefty tip, and hit the streets once more.

After a delicious meal, everything always seemed brighter to Erin. She knew it was only a figment of her imagination brought on by some prehistoric sense of comfort, but she relished in it all the same. Especially after everything she'd been through the last three years. She clung to that feeling, closed off from the world around her, lost in thought. Rounding a corner, she ran into something hard and warm that brought her crashing back down to the real world. Strong arms snaked around her to keep her from falling to the ground.

"Oh, I'm so sorry," Erin said to the broad chest that dominated her view. "I wasn't paying attention."

The chest rumbled with a chuckle as a familiar voice answered back. "That's quite all right; I'm used to beautiful women throwing themselves at me."

Erin looked up into the smiling face of Detective Remy Mercier. Her face burned with what … she couldn't be sure. "Detective! I'm sorry."

Remy winked, releasing Erin and taking a step back. "Now, I believe I told you to call me Remy, Miss Erin."

Erin took a step back, putting more space between her and the detective. The food in her stomach rebelled, making her feel a bit queasy. Remy's carefree demeanor fell when he noticed her discomfort. He took another step back. Erin found that she could breathe a little easier.

"How's your investigation going?" Remy asked, tucking his hands into his pockets, adopting a nonchalant demeanor.

She didn't bother asking him how he knew. He probably had her tailed as soon as she left his office. "Just fine," she snapped, walking around him, a brisk step in her walk. Better to be angry than unsure. And with the detective, she was unsure of how she felt.

Remy's long legs easily caught up with her, much to her dismay. He looked down at her expectantly. Erin sighed; he would find out eventually anyway. "I'm going to talk to Jacque Déco later this evening. She's willing to talk to me about my sister's actions before her disappearance." Remy stopped short, staring with his mouth open.

"What is it about you and your sister?" he demanded, incredulous.

"What do you mean?"

Remy closed the space between them in two strides. He was just tall enough that Erin had to crane her neck slightly to look him in the eye. And when she did, she found it suddenly hard to breathe properly. Perhaps it was the way the sunlight danced off his coppery hair, bringing out the shades of gold and red. Or perhaps it was the way he smelled, clean and smoky, that reminded her too much of someone else.

"First, your sister comes along and befriends Jacque like it's nothing," Remy went on, completely unaware of the turmoil raging inside Erin's heart. "Then you come up, and she's suddenly willing to talk to you."

"So?" Erin snipped.

"Jacqueline Déco is not known to be overfriendly or helpful to anyone," Remy pointed out. "I have a gut feeling that she's holding something back, but I couldn't get past her walls. So, what makes you and your sister different?"

"No one, and I mean *no one*, can resist my sister. She's that likable," Erin said, holding up a finger. "And *I* can be pretty persuasive when I need to be. Now if you'll excuse me, I'm heading back to my hotel. I need to check in on my mother. She worries."

Erin spun on her heel and walked as fast as she could back to the hotel without slipping into a full-on sprint, her mind whirling all the way. The last thing she needed was for anyone to get suspicious of the true nature of her sister's disappearance, especially attractive-looking detectives. Erin shook her head, dispelling the treacherous thoughts. She wasn't attracted to Remy Mercier, who was beyond a doubt a shameless flirt and womanizer. No, it was just her body reacting to a male presence. She hasn't had any sort of physical contact with a male since Caleb, nor has she had the desire to. All she needed to do was take a shower and get some rest.

Back in her room, Erin released a heavy sigh, looking longingly at her bed. But she couldn't throw herself at it just yet. She really should have done this her first night in town but had been too tired to even begin to think about performing that level of magic. From her bag, she pulled out two black and two white stones. She placed them in opposite corners of her room while chanting quietly under her breath. In her mind's eye, a white light flowed from her hand to each stone, imbuing them with a golden light until the entire room shone. The line flashed briefly before fading, but the protection lingered. Now she had a safe place to retreat to, a place where no one could get to her either physically or magically.

She kicked off her shoes, falling face-first into her pillows. Her body sank into the bed, almost sighing in relief. She buried her face in her pillow, savoring the pleasant scent of soap and sea air. A small smile drifted across her face as she fell deep into the realm of sleep.

The small boat rocked gently as the current carried it onward to some unknown location completely surrounded by a fog so thick that one was tempted to cut it with a knife. Erin sat up calmly and peered into the fog around her but couldn't discern either her location or the time of day. The only things she could see was the cool fog mist and the murky water that her tiny boat glided on. As she continued to stare out across the water, large looming shadows emerged. When her tiny craft neared the massive, semi-ominous shadows, their true form became clearer—giant cypress trees, with their limbs reaching out like so many spindly fingers eager to touch the inky waters below. Spanish moss hung from every branch, occasionally touching the water in some places. With a gasp, Erin realized that she was floating down a bayou. And though nothing around her gave her any indication about which one of the numerous bayous in southern Louisiana, she knew, deep down, that it was close to Moonbay. She strained her senses to learn more about where she was, but not a sound could be heard other than the small waves cresting away from her boat. She wished she had more light. Perhaps then she might be able to see her surrounds better, find some sort of landmark or sign that would help her find it again when she returned to the waking world.

She registered a weight in her hand and discovered, much to her surprise, that she now held a lantern. A flash of green sparked to life inside the lantern and grew until it cast its eerie light farther than a normal lantern should have. The green light gave the peaceful surroundings a new sinister feeling to them. *Perhaps the light was a bad idea,* Erin thought and doused the light. Something rustled around on the shoreline, and for the first time since she found herself on this strange journey, Erin felt the first twinges of fear. If she wasn't careful, she, too, might end up captive like her sister. Her wards only protected her physical body, not her spiritual one.

Erin gripped the edges of her boat tightly, scanning both banks for what stirred just beyond her sight. As she strained her ears, she could have sworn she heard a slight hissing sound, followed by something heavy dragging along the ground.

Without warning, the world around her exploded into a blinding white light that caused Erin to cry out in alarm, throwing her arms up to shield her head. She threw her body down to the floor of her watercraft. She braced for an attack that would never come.

The ringing of her cell phone jerked Erin out of her slumber. She was torn between relief and frustration. Relief over not having to face down her sister's captures for a while longer and frustration at not finding the answers she sought. Erin reached for her purse, blindly digging around for her phone. It was her mother.

"Still alive, mom," Erin joked, stifling a yawn.

"Very funny," chided her mother. "Found anything out yet?"

"Nuh-uh. I've only been here two days. Plus, I'm basically starting from scratch. I do have a lead that I'm checking out later. I'll call you after that. How are things on your end?"

"Pretty much the same. Your friend Orrin called to check in on us. He's such a sweet young man. I'm glad you two are friends. I worry about you all alone on the other side of the world."

"I can take care of myself, mom," Erin groaned. She glanced at the clock and cursed. "Look, mom, I got to go. It's almost time for me to meet up with my contact. I'll call you in a couple of days, OK?"

"Be safe, baby," urged her mother.

Erin promised that she would. She ran her fingers through her hair, soothing down the worst of the bed head, grabbed her purse and bolted out the door. She drove as fast as she dared towards the garage where she hoped Jacque was waiting for her.

Jacque was leaning up against the closed garage, smoking a cigarette, when Erin drove up. Instead of grease-stained coverall, Jacque wore ripped jeans and a simple white tank top. She must have just gotten off of work because she still had some grease on her face, and her hair was still up in a bun like before. Erin let out the breath that she had held for the last two blocks. Jacque flicked the cigarette off to the side and approached the car.

"Leave your car here," she told Erin.

Bemused, Erin complied. "How come?"

Jacque made a noncommittal gesture. "Where we're going, parking's a pain to find. It's faster to just walk from here." She turned and walked down a side street, not turning to see if Erin would follow. Erin frowned as she scurried to catch up.

It didn't take her long to catch up to the other woman, who was visibly uncomfortable. Erin decided to take a stab at some small talk to hopefully ease the tension between them and perhaps show Jacque that she wasn't as bad as she behaved during their first meeting.

"So how exactly did you and Laura meet?"

Jacque sighed, closing her eyes in a manner that gave Erin the impression that she was praying for strength. "One of the trucks broke down, and I was the only mechanic crazy enough to go all the way out there and fix it. While I was working, Laura came up and started talking. At first, I didn't pay her any mind." A muscle feathered in her jaw. "I don't care for people. They all want something from you and give nothing back in return. I told myself a long time ago that it wasn't worth the drama, so I keep to myself."

Erin nodded. She understood Jacque's sentiment. She, too, had felt the very same way when she had been forced to leave behind all that she knew in order to be safe and free. But it was a very lonely way to live. She felt a pang of sadness for Jacque. At least Erin managed to carve out a bit of happiness for herself; clearly, Jacque had not. No wonder Laura had been drawn to the woman sulking ahead of her.

"Well, she kept on talking to me, and before I realized what happened, I had agreed to grab a drink with her," Jacque said, shaking her head. Erin came abreast to her and noted the small smile on Jacque's face. "For some crazy reason, I kept that promise and well, after that," Jacque shrugged, "I'd guess you call us friends."

Erin let out a small laugh. "That sounds like Laura."

The pair walked in silence for a while. Erin remained silent. She could tell that Jacque wanted to tell her more but felt like she couldn't. Back in Dorshire, Erin was a teacher, and if that profession taught her anything, it was that sometimes silence was the best way to get information out of someone, especially if they felt guilty.

It finally became too much for Jacque to bear. She stopped abruptly and spun around and stared Erin right in the eyes. "Your sister showed me her magic too." Erin's face remained neutral. "When I asked her why she would do something like that, she said that it was because she could tell that I had it too."

Erin cocked her head to one side. She reached out with her magic but felt nothing from the other woman. If she had magic, she hid it extremely well.

"I can't see it," she confessed. The tension in Jacque's shoulders eased.

"Good, I was worried that I was getting complacent. Perhaps your sister's sight is stronger than yours." She started walking again, leaving a very confused Erin in her wake.

"Hold on a moment!" Erin shouted, chasing after Jacque. "Care to explain that a bit more?"

Jacque huffed. "I have magic, but I can't … won't use it."

"Why?"

Erin's question went unanswered. Jacque's walls were once again firmly in place. Erin sighed and let it go. She wasn't there to unravel the mysteries of Jacqueline Déco.

They turned a corner and walked down another quiet street. Modest houses sat on well-manicured lawns with minimal but tasteful landscaping. Only one house stood out against the neutral colored homes. The exterior color palate would not have been out of place in the main strip where Erin's hotel resided, but on the quiet street, it stood out like an exotic bird among finches. Wind chimes and sun catchers claimed nearly every available inch on the front porch, creating a musical light show whenever the wind blew. Much of the yard in the front of the house was taken up by a neat but extensive garden. Erin recognized some of the herbs in it, and her excitement grew. At the end of the driveway sat a nondescript little white sign that simply read *Miss Eulalie's*.

Erin had no clue who or what Miss Eulalie was. Apparently, for locals, her name was enough. Jacque trudged up the driveway. With each laboring step, her shoulders rolled inward, her head drooped. Whoever this Miss Eulalie was, she was someone who Jacque was not happy to see today.

Jacque disappeared through the vibrant purple door, leaving it wide open for Erin to follow through. As she crossed the threshold, she felt a small wave of something caress her. It didn't feel threatening or harmful, more curious than anything, like a dog sniffing at her. It reminded her a bit of the wards around her home. Her excitement grew. This definitely was the house of a magic user.

Erin looked about the front room, drinking in everything around her. The front room bore a strong resemblance to a waiting room. Several plush chairs filled the space, with small tables between them. On the small tables sat some much-handled magazines. The only difference was the smell inside the house. Instead of smelling strongly of sanitizing chemicals, the room had a slightly spicy aroma, followed by the faintest hint of incense smoke.

There were two doorways on the other end of the waiting room. The one on the left was covered by a beaded curtain, while the one on the right remained unobstructed. Through the opening, Erin glimpsed a small but tidy kitchen. Clearly, no one was in the kitchen. Erin turned to walk through the beaded doorway but stopped when Jacque placed her hand on her shoulder. Erin looked back at her. Jacque shook her head, dropping her hand.

"Not through there," she said. "Only paying customers go through there." Jacque led Erin through the doorway that led to the kitchen.

The kitchen was immaculate. Not a speck of dirt or blackened smug marred any of the surfaces. Everything was white, right down to the laminate flooring. The only splashes of color came from the herbs that grew along the windowsill. It was a sharp contrast to Erin's kitchen, with its warm and welcoming colors that gave off a homey feel to it. Miss Eulalie's kitchen was sterile and industrial.

Jacque grabbed a beer from the refrigerator, silently offering it to Erin—who shook her head. Jacque shrugged and cracked the beer open and then proceeded to chug it down in a few gulps.

The gentle hiss of beads drew Erin's attention back towards the waiting room. She spied two women as she peered around the corner. One woman was tall and slender, dressed elegantly. Her bleach blonde hair was cut and styled meticulously. She reached into her designer purse and pulled out a small roll of bills, which she handed to the other woman. The other woman was an elderly black woman with silvery dreadlocks. Her amber eyes narrowed in on the other woman as she took the money from her. With her other hand, she extended something Erin couldn't see towards the blonde woman.

"The charm can only do so much for you," the older woman who had to be Miss Eulalie told the bleached blonde woman. "Some things cannot be fixed, even with magic. If you want my advice, if you're worried that your husband's having an affair, talk to him."

The bleached blonde woman's lips tightened into a thin white line, and she turned to leave. Her icy eyes narrowed on Erin and Jacque who stood in the doorway to the kitchen—silent intruders. The blonde woman snatched the charm out of Eulalie's hand and stormed out of the house without a word, slamming the door as she went.

"Prissy bitch," Eulalie sneered, shaking her head. "Whatever you need must be important if you're here, Jacque." The old woman ambled towards them. Her shrewd eyes raked over Erin, briefly scanning her from head to toe. Erin shuttered. She felt laid bare by the old woman's gaze. "It's been a while since you've come to visit your old grandmamma."

Erin's eyes widened and flew back and forth between the two women. Their eyes were the same color and shape. The shape of their face was similar as well. It was there that the similarities ended. Jacque was darker than her grandmother, coffee to her grandmother's caramel. Jacque also had several inches over her grandmother, who now was studying Erin intently.

"Erin, meet my grandmamma, Eulalie Déco, the voodoo queen of Moonbay Bayou."

Erin bobbed her head respectfully. Eulalie's amber eyes narrowed as she studied her granddaughter and Erin.

"I don't know about you, Miss Erin," Eulalie said with a sigh, "but I need a drink."

Erin stood aside to let the older woman pass. She was surprised to see the old woman pull out a glass decanter full of amber liquid. Eulalie poured about a knuckle's worth of the amber liquid into a small glass and tossed it back with practiced ease.

Without warning, Eulalie lashed out, sending a magical barrage barreling towards Erin. Erin flinched as she hastily and sloppily threw up her shields. Jacque looked on, sympathetic, while Eulalie carried on like nothing was happening. Erin felt a sliver of fear race down her spine. This was the most powerful practitioner she had ever come across. Not even Connor had this much power. As suddenly as the assault started, it ended. Erin cautiously lowered her shields.

She swallowed, finally understanding why Jacque was so reluctant to come here in the first place. "Thank you for agreeing to see me today, Mrs. Déco."

The old woman laughed. "I didn't agree to a thing, sweetie. My darling granddaughter sulking over there in the corner doesn't know how to use a phone. She just pops in at random ... whenever she remembers I'm alive."

"Not now, grandmamma," Jacque groaned. "You know my reasons for the distance. Anyway, we're not here to talk about me."

"That we aren't," Eulalie stated matter-of-factly. "You're here because of that missing little white girl."

"My sister," Erin cut in. "Now I know my sister came to you for help. Did she make it? What did you tell her?"

Irritation flashed in the older woman's amber eyes, eyes that reminded Erin of birds of prey. "Yes, your sister came to me, asking all sorts of questions a girl like her shouldn't. I told her to stay out of it 'cause it wasn't her fight." The ire in Eulalie's eyes faded into pity. "Clearly, she didn't listen to me. They never do." She refilled her glass, studying Erin once again. She grabbed another glass and poured another round. "You English witches are all the same. Always so eager to throw yourself into the fray without any thought about whether or not you should."

Erin bit down the retort on her tongue and said instead, "Actually, we're Irish."

Again, ire flashed in Eulalie's eyes, this time accompanied by simmering magic. Erin figured that she wasn't used to people questioning her, challenging her in any fashion. Erin knew she was being silly since she needed

Eulalie's cooperation to find her sister, but there was something about the older woman that set her hackles up.

Jacque shifted uncomfortably in the corner, breaking the tension in the air. Erin backed down, and the fire ebbed out of Eulalie's eyes.

"Here," Eulalie said, holding out the other glass to Erin, "you're gonna need this since it's clear you won't listen to me either."

"Thank you," Erin said, accepting the glass. She brought it up to her nose and gently sniffed. The pleasantly spicy aroma of rum filled her nose. It tasted as good as it smelled.

"Don't thank me yet," Eulalie countered as she walked back out into her waiting room.

FIVE

EULALIE SETTLED INTO a crimson wingback chair, rearranging the folds of her dress. Erin and Jacque stood awkwardly in the kitchen until Eulalie beckoned them to join her with an imperious wave. The two women crossed the room, one more reluctant than the other. Jacque chose to sit as far from her grandmother as she could, perching on the edge of an ottoman just outside the kitchen. Erin chose a simple chair near enough to Eulalie to hear but with enough space that both women could breathe. For a while, the only sound in the parlor came from the antique cuckoo clock that hung from the wall.

"There is light and dark in everything," Eulalie said at last, breaking the silence, "even in magic. Some only follow the light, some only follow the dark, and some ... well some of us do a bit of both." Erin tried to not fidget in her seat. She hadn't come here to hear stuff that she already knew. What she wanted to hear was what her sister had attempted to hunt down with this woman's help.

The older woman sighed, fiddling with the end of one of her dreadlocks. "Your sister came to me some time ago to find the source of the accidents at the work sights. She suspected that a local had something to do with it. I told her that there was no one in town who would do something like that." A wry smile crept across Eulalie's face. "Your sister then asked about those who live in the bayous along the tributaries. Sharp as a whip, that sister of yours." Erin smiled back. She knew. "Of course she was right, the person who's responsible for the attacks on the work sights and your sister's disappearance doesn't live in town, hasn't for many years."

Erin leaned forward in her chair, focused on Eulalie and her story. She didn't bother to hide the hunger from her eyes. She *needed* to hear the name, needed to know who took her sister.

Eulalie took another sip of her drink before answering. "Sébastien Villére."

Jacque leaped up from her seat and stormed back into the kitchen. Erin could hear a cabinet door small and the distinct sound of the stopper being removed from the glass decanter. Just who was this man?

"That was his name when he was a simple voodoo practitioner, powerful but just one of many. Now he goes by the name The Night King." Eulalie scoffed into her drink. "He grew up in a poor family and hungered for the power and wealth of others. He always hated anyone who had something better than him—better job, better house, car, money, all the same to him. That hunger turned him towards the dark. He became cruel and ruthless. But he was also charismatic, and people flocked to him in droves. He lives out there in the bayous, somewhere. He claimed that territory after the hurricane and no doubt is trying to drive off anyone who's trying to bring people back into the land he now thinks is his."

"So, you don't know how I can reach him?"

Eulalie shook her head. "He is beyond you, girlie. The only thing you can do is mourn your sister—because she's never coming back—and go home."

Erin sat back affronted. "I could no sooner do that than fly across the sky. I'm not leaving this backwater town until I have my sister or die trying. It is not in my family to just sit idly by while innocent people are suffering. I am a Guardian, sworn to defend those who cannot fight against the dark forces in our world."

She found herself standing, glaring down at the other woman. She hadn't even registered the motion. All she felt was immense rage and frustration. Here this woman was, telling her that she should just give up on her sister, ignore an evil that *she* has allowed to fester in her town. Sparks dance along her fingertips. The lights flicker, and the multitude of small objects shutter at the wake of Erin's rage. Eulalie remained unfazed. Erin took several calming breaths, letting her anger go. She would get no further help from this woman at all if she destroyed her house.

"Please," Erin begged through gritted teeth, "I understand that I don't know anything about your town or the way your people use magic. But this is my blood. I cannot walk away. Please help me."

"No."

Stunned Erin fell back into her seat. "Why the hell not?"

Eulalie swelled up. "I don't have to answer to a witchling a quarter of my age. You might be a big shot where you're from, but this," she waved her hands wide, "this is my domain, and I will not have you questioning my motives or looking down your nose at me." Her eyes flashed a brilliant gold, and something cold and foreign seeped into Erin's body.

She couldn't move, couldn't push the foreign force out. It sped along her body, claiming every last bit of it for Eulalie whose eyes still burned with a golden fire. Her lungs labored against the force, and panic set in, a wild primal panic that chased away all rational thought, every scrap of training and skill, leaving only the most primal of thoughts—to break free. From the corner of her bulging eye, Erin saw Jacque return to the waiting room. She took one look and Erin and dropped her glass, shattering it on the hardwood floors. The cold fire burned its way through Erin's mind, taking total control over her body. Darkness crept into the edges of her vision. Tears ran unhindered down her face as she stared at Jacque, silently pleading for her to do something. Help her in some way. Jacque's own tears were the last thing Erin saw before her world faded completely into darkness.

With a gasp, Erin regained control of her body once more. She gulped the air greedily, frantically looking around for the wicked old witch who had placed that terrifying spell on her. She was surprised to find that she wasn't in Eulalie's house of horrors anymore but in her car where she left it what felt like hours ago. As the daylight faded, Erin regained more of her senses. She scanned her body for any signs of damage or lingering spell work. She felt nothing, but that didn't ease her worries. She would have to perform a cleansing on herself when she got back home—just to be safe. Erin gripped the steering wheel with white knuckles. Half of her demanded that she go back to that old witch's house and seek retribution against the unprovoked attack, but that was only a small part. The larger, logical portion of her brain urged her to leave it be. She got a name and a generalized location. That was more than enough for her to work with. Listening to that part, Erin started her car and drove back into town, stopping at the first bar she came across. She needed a drink, or three.

From the outside, the bar didn't look like much. The worn planks that made up its exterior were flaked with several layers of old paint. The only paint that looked fresh was the bright blue door. Perhaps the proprietor designed it that way, perhaps not. Either way, the bright blue door urged Erin to walk through it and join the rest of the patrons inside.

Erin parked her car and pocketed her keys. If she had one too many, the bar was only a couple of blocks from her hotel, so she could walk home.

String lights ran the length of the overhang that covered the outdoor seating area. A few patrons lounged in the metal chairs smoking, drinking, and laughing. They paid no attention to Erin as she walked up, too wrapped up in their own conversations. Erin tried to pull comfort from the normalcy of it all. Her nerves were still raw from her encounter with Eulalie. She felt drawn to the light, laughter, and music that poured out from the windows of the bar. She let the high energy surrounding the establishment chase away the last vestiges of her fear. She released it into the night with a sigh. Not all of it left. In her chest, some lingering tightness remained. She planned on drowning it thoroughly.

Inside was just as crowded as the noise suggested, leaving Erin no option but to weave her way through the crowd to get to the bar. As she tries to get the bartender's attention, she listens to the commotion around her. There was a comforting familiarity to the noise around her. It reminded her of the pub back home or the clubs she and her college friends used to visit. Places like this transcend all barriers of time and space. Everyone wants to have a good time.

She finally managed to snag the haggard bartender's attention long enough to order a beer. When her drink was placed in front of her, she quickly moved out of the way before some other patron could elbow her. She then scanned the crowded space in vain for a place to sit and process her visit with Eulalie Déco. As luck would have it, she spied one unoccupied seat in a dark little corner that suited her needs perfectly. Safely tucked away into the shadows, she watched the vibrant people around her, missing the days when her life had been a little simpler, and she didn't have the burdens she did now.

As more people filed into the bar, the temperature in the room rose. The ceiling fans that whirled furiously from the rafters did nothing more than circulate the muggy air. Sweat formed at the back of Erin's neck, making her wish for the cool sweet nighttime breezes that would alleviate the heat. But sitting in the back of the bar like she was, it was very unlikely that she would ever feel them.

Erin signaled for a refill to the waitress that maneuvered through the crowd with practiced ease, cleaning up and taking orders. She nodded to Erin, indicating that she saw her, and continued on with her rounds. The band struck up a lively tune, and there was a rush, as people either dragged their partners to the middle of the floor or moved to get out of the way.

Erin watched the couples with a smile on her face. She let her thoughts wander to the point that she didn't notice that she was no longer alone at her table.

"Long day?" asked a familiar voice.

Startled, Erin jumped in her seat, earning a laugh from the handsome Detective Remy Mercier. His charming smile and friendly face brought out a smile from her.

"You might say that."

"I take it your meeting with Jacqueline Déco didn't go well?"

Erin suppressed a shudder. "You might say that."

He frowned, shifting from friend to police in a single breath. "What happened?"

"I met her grandmother Eulalie."

Remy shivered in his seat, mirroring her sentiment over the old woman exactly. "You are one very lucky lady. That woman has a mean streak that would make the devil himself cry for his mamma."

The waitress returned, setting the fresh beer on the table, taking away the empty bottle. She flashed Remy a flirtatious smile that he returned easily with a roguish wink. She blushed and sauntered back out into the crowd.

"I believe that," Erin snorted, taking a long gulp of her drink.

"Bit of local legend for you," Remy said, leaning in close. Whether it was her still frayed nerves or the scent of his cologne, Erin's body shivered at the closeness. "She descended from one of the most famous voodoo queens in *all* Louisiana. She got enough power that she could run this whole town if she wanted to. She doesn't like people sticking their noses in her business, and she hates the police.

Most officers keep a healthy distance from Miss Eulalie Déco."

"What about you?"

Remy flashed Erin a smile that undoubtedly led to many a heartbreak. Her own treacherous heart fluttered like a captured bird within her chest. She had never been one for casual one-night stands, but the detective certainly helped her to see the benefits of such interactions.

"Well, like any good bayou boy, I was brought up with a healthy respect for the supernatural. When I have to deal with Miss Eulalie, I *always* come with a gift and my irresistible charm."

Erin snorted into her drink, and the conversation turned to more pleasant topics. Remy told her one hilarious tale after another, each one more ridiculous than the last and undoubtedly untrue to the last syllable. But they helped her to forget about her fear and anger over Eulalie and the constant gnawing worry over the fate of her sister. The burden of being a Guardian and the matriarch of her family melted away, leaving only her, a woman who was in the company of a charming man. In turn, Erin told him about her life in Ireland, obviously leaving out the magical parts.

Round after round, they downed until Erin's world was lost in a drunken haze. They drank, danced, laughed, and then drank some more. The other patrons of the bar came and went. In the company of the ever-amiable Remy, Erin felt like she was safely encircled by lifelong friends. She hadn't felt this unfetter in ages—perhaps ever.

Erin excused herself for the restroom, swaying to the beat of the music in the air and in her blood. Upon her return, she spied a gorgeous and buxomest redhead plying her wiles on Remy, who was all too eager to play along. Erin grinned fiendishly, not because she was jealous but because she felt comfortable enough with Remy now to tease him about his taste in women.

Remy spied Erin's unsteady return to their table and disentangled himself from the redhead and kissed the back of her hand. "See you later, ma chér," he said as his kissed her hand. He intercepted Erin and steered her towards the bar.

"She seemed nice," Erin teased, grinning from ear to ear.

"I'm with the only woman a man could possibly want tonight," Remy countered, throwing his arm around Erin's shoulders.

Erin giggled and patted Remy's chest. "Oh, you are good. I bet you have all the girls chasing you. Though it's kinda hard to trust a man who flirts with every passing skirt that catches his eye."

Remy looked down at Erin with a strange expression on his face. "I don't mean anything by it. There's nothing wrong with a little harmless flirting."

"Oh no, don't worry your pretty little head over it," Erin assured him. "I don't care in the slightest. But just out of curiosity, how would a girl know if you're serious or not?"

Remy shrugged. "I've never met a woman that made me want to be serious. So, your guess is as good as mine."

"I think that the right person would make you want to be better," Erin commented as she hoisted herself onto the bar stool. "That's what he did for me."

"Who?"

Erin shook her head as a wave of anguish, and guilt crashed over her. She felt her eyes burn and her throat tighten. She tried to swallow the felling down. She would not be one of those people sobbing in a bar over their lost love.

A waitress placed two beers on the bar in front of them. Remy held his up in the air. "Here's to meeting someone who makes us better!" Erin smiled weakly but raised her drink all the same. Seeing the turn in her mood, Remy hauled Erin to the nearest pool table where he tried and failed to teach her how to play. But it did make her forget about the man who made her want to be a better person and a stronger Guardian—at least for now.

Erin gulped the night air greedily. After spending all night inside the bar, the cool breezes that wafted off the water were sweeter than any elixir she'd ever tasted. It helped to clear her head slightly.

"All right, love," Remy said, throwing Erin's arm over his shoulder while his other hand snaked around her waist, shifting most of her weight onto him, "I think it's past time for you to go to bed."

Erin grinned up at him with her eyes closed. "I think you're right, officer. Take me away." She dissolved into a fit of giggles, barely able to catch her breath. Remy chuckled and half-carried her down the street.

The street lights wavered and glistened in Erin's drunken haze. She swung her arm around aimlessly in an attempt to catch the pretty balls of light around her. Remy deftly kept her steady and out of any oncoming traffic. As they walked through the glittering night towards Erin's hotel, her thoughts, as muddled as they were, drifted back to her sister. Guilt crashed into her. Here she was, roaring drunk, while her sister was most likely suffering at the hands of a dark voodoo practitioner in some godforsaken corner of a swamp.

"You all right?" Remy asked, once again in tune with her mood. Erin remained silent, blankly staring ahead at the sidewalk, trying to not break completely down. "Worried about your sister?" Erin managed a small nod. Remy stopped walking and spun her gently around so that they faced each other. He pulled her in for a tight embrace. Erin buried her nose into the crook of his neck, breathing in his scent deeply. All the pain, guilt and unease drifted away like smoke on the wind. She lingered in the safety of

Remy's arms until she had enough control over her emotions. She gave him a watery smile, silently thanking him for being there for her. Remy brought a hand up to Erin's face and gently wiped away a stray tear.

"I promise you, Erin, I *will* find your sister and return her to you." Erin looked into Remy's eyes and saw his true self. He would do whatever it took to keep his promise to her. That's who he was. He was a protector the same as she. Erin offered him a small smile, and the pair resumed walking.

The full effect of the night came crashing in on Erin the moment they came upon her hotel. Her stomach and the world rolled and tumbled, making her feel queasy. She was ever grateful for Remy's arm around her, the one steady thing in her life at that moment.

In the elevator, Erin yawned, leaning against Remy, savoring the heat of his body and the safety she felt in his arms. Her eyelids grew heavy and refused to stay open, not even when the elevator reached her floor and the door opened. She allowed herself to be led along down the hallway to her room. She withdrew her key from her pocket, holding it out for him. She didn't protest when he propped her up against the wall while he unlocked her door.

She slid to the floor, fully prepared to go to sleep right where she was.

"Not yet, darlin'," Remy chuckled, hoisting her up with a small grunt. He picked Erin up bridal style and carried her over to her bed. She giggled as her world swam again. He then gently laid her on it, removing only her light jacket and shoes.

Erin snuggled into the pillows, a sleepy smile on her face. Remy covered her with a throw blanket, shaking his head slightly at the intoxicated woman on the bed.

"You're the best, Remy," Erin murmured into her pillows. "But I hope I find Laura before you do."

"And why is that?" he asked with a laugh.

"Because she's being held by a dark practitioner, and you don't have magic like we do. You might end up a slave or something."

Remy stilled, a frown breaking out across his face. He wanted to ask Erin what she meant by that, but she had already fallen asleep, snoring softly. He chewed over her words for a moment longer before disregarding them as drunken nonsense. But being the type of detective he was, he wouldn't throw them out entirely. Perhaps he would bring them up again when Erin's mind was a bit more sober. Quietly, he filled a glass with water and placed it on the bedside table next to a small bottle of aspirin before letting himself out of Erin's room, making sure to lock the door behind him.

SIX

SOME EVIL LITTLE gremlin somehow had managed to get past Erin's wards to only beat heavily on a drum, for whatever reason. Try as she might, she couldn't ignore the pounding that she felt within her own skull. Admitting defeat, she opened her eyes and sat up, determined to kill the gremlin; only there was not one. The pounding in her head was the result of her colossal hangover from the night before. Her stomach rolled in defiance as she swung her feet to the floor. Erin took several deep breaths, willing her stomach to calm while promising to never ... *never* drink that much again. The pounding in her head intensified when someone decided it was a good idea to make a social call by pounding on her door.

Erin groaned, raising her hands to her face, dragging them down. With extreme caution, she turned her head and nearly wept in relief when she saw that someone, most likely Remy, had left a glass of water and bottle of aspirin by her bed. She uncapped the bottle, spilling out the little white pills that would ease the pressure in her head. She downed them with the entire glass of water and waited for her stomach to recoil and settle before she dared to get out of bed. Once the water settled into her stomach without the threat of coming back up, she shuffled her way across the room to the door. She flung it open with more force than necessary, fully intending to tell the person on the other side off, when she registered who was standing on her doorstep.

Jacqueline Deco.

Surprise, confusion, and anger fought for control inside Erin's alcohol-weakened mind. However, the events of the day before gave anger the leverage it needed to win out as the dominant emotion. Erin gripped the frame of the doorway tightly, wood crackling beneath her fingers.

"You better have a damn good reason for being here," she gritted out. "I came to you for *help*, not to be taken advantage of and violated! You knew what I was walking into and didn't think to warn me at all. I could have been prepared, could have gone about it a completely different way! But no; let's just let the foreign witch suffer for no good reason!"

Jacque remained silent throughout Erin's ranting, taking it all without complaint. Erin sighed, not having the energy to maintain her anger. It fizzled out, leaving her more exhausted than before. She rubbed her face again, groaning. It was too early for all this. Yet Jacque still stood in front of her door.

"What do you want?" she asked, voice dull and listless. All she wanted to do was go back to bed and sleep off a bit of her hangover.

Jacque shifted from foot to foot, clearly uncomfortable. "Can I come in? I want to talk but not out in the open like this."

Erin sighed and rolled her eyes before stepping aside to let the young woman into the room. Jacque walked into the middle of the room, looking every bit as awkward as the day before. Erin took a small amount of pleasure from the other woman's discomfort. She should feel bad about what she put Erin through with that demon masquerading as human named Eulalie.

"Do you mind if I wash up?" Erin asked with a sigh when it became evident that Jacque wasn't ready to speak yet.

Jacque jumped when Erin spoke. Her head jerked in a manner that could have been a nod if it had not been so stiff. "Go ahead." Jacque settled on the couch, instantly retreating into her thoughts. Erin shrugged and left her there.

Erin stood in the shower, letting the near-scalding water beat her body into a state of relaxation. The longer she stood under the water, the clearer her head became. She didn't quite remember how she got home last night but was immensely grateful that she had stumbled into Detective Mercier and not some random guy. Who knows what could have happened? Creeps are everywhere and are all too eager to take advantage of anyone who doesn't have a completely clear head. Eventually, the temperature of the water began to drop, and Erin knew that she now had to face the woman sitting in her living space. She moaned but turned off the water and toweled off.

Steam billowed out of the bathroom the second Erin opened the door, letting all the delicious heat waft out into the rest of the room. Wrapped snuggly in a bathrobe, she dragged a brush through her tangled locks as she walked out.

Jacque had moved from the sofa to the kitchen where she busied herself by making a pot of tea. From the aroma that wafted from the teapot, Erin suspected that it was herbal. She eyed the pot and the woman suspiciously.

"What's in the pot?"

Jacque arched a brow at Erin's sharp tone. "Herbs."

This time, it was Erin's turn to raise a brow. "Magic herbs?"

"Anyone can use herbs without having to resort to magic," Jacque snipped.

Erin gave her a dubious look as she walked across the room to where her clothes were. Jacque turned around respectfully. She dressed quickly, pulling on a pair of shorts and a tank top. She cleared her throat, letting Jacque know that she was decent. The other woman poured the steaming, slightly green liquid into a small mug, leaving it on the counter. Erin stared at the glass, pondering whether or not it was worth the risk to drink it. She got the feeling that if she accepted the drink, then she was, in part, forgiving Jacque. She chewed in the side of her cheek, debating. Discretely, she reached out with her magic to test the cup. She felt no spells, but that didn't mean it was safe; there are numerous herbs that can hurt you without magic. She felt a gentle push in the back of her mind that urged her to give the young mechanic a second chance. She realized that the push came from her deceased great-grandmother Elise who appeared now and again to point Erin in the right direction.

The heat from the mug seeped into Erin's fingers as they wrapped around it. A slight floral aroma rose up with the steam. It smelled pleasant. She took a tentative sip— light, sweet, and calming. She took another, larger sip. Hot liquid cascaded down her throat, chasing away the effects of her hangover.

Eyes wide, she saluted Jacque with the mug. "Impressive, and I need this recipe."

That earned a smile from the younger woman. "It was my mother's recipe, but my grandmother made it the most growing up."

"Did you grow up with your mom and grandmother?"

Jacque's smile faded, and she shook her head. "No. Eulalie raised me. I don't have any memories of my mother. If it wasn't for the few photos I found in the attic, I wouldn't even know what she looked like."

Erin felt a rush of compassion for Jacque who took a steadying breath before plunging into the reason why she had shown up on Erin's doorstep.

"My grandmother and I don't always see eye to eye. I need you to understand that when I took you to see her, I thought she would help, but clearly, I was wrong. I'm sorry about that." Erin felt the urge to reach out and touch Jacque, but she knew that the other woman wouldn't respond well to that. Instead, Erin toasted her with her mug, letting the other woman know that she had forgiven her. Jacque gave Erin a small half smile while her eyes flashed briefly with relief before becoming sad.

"I have magic like my grandmother, like my mother … like my father, but I don't use it. I refuse to. I've fought with my grandmother over this many times, but I will not budge. Eulalie is my father's mother. He grew up with all this hate in his heart. Hate over being different. Hate over how the townspeople treated people like him and his mother. Hate over having nothing while some people seemed to have everything. Well, one day, he had enough and started to use his power to get a leg up over people. At first, it was small things like a job or a car or a date, but eventually, he used it to claw his way up the ladder politically.

"The people who were like us saw his rise to power and flocked to him like he was the Messiah, my mother included. They quickly fell in love and became the uncontested king and queen of the bayou. Eventually, my mother got pregnant, and suddenly, it was like the veil had been lifted from her eyes. She saw my father for what he truly was—a cruel, vindictive man who loved no one but himself and the power he gained. She realized that she didn't want her child to grow up in a world like that, so she fled to the only place she knew she would be safe—Eulalie's. Her parents had died in a car crash when she was young. She grew up in foster care until she aged out. Eulalie helped her get settled when she first came down here." Jacque shrugged a shoulder. "Anyway, she knew my father would never attack his own mother. Eulalie is stronger than her son and my mother combined. I always wondered why she never stepped up sooner and stopped my dad from doing what he did. By the time she got her mind around to doing something, it was too late."

Jacque stopped, staring ahead, seeing nothing. Erin didn't press her. If she wanted to continue her story, then she would, though Erin had an inkling as to where it was headed.

"When my mom left, the spell my dad had over his followers broke. People started leaving him left and right. Plenty still stayed, those who relish the dark, but they didn't number as many as those who left. My father lost face with each person who left, which was something that he couldn't stomach at all. He planned his revenge against my mother from his hideout, waiting for her to give birth. He wouldn't dare to harm his own bloodline. He needed me to secure his lineage." Jacque's face contorted as if she had swallowed something bitter.

"Shortly after I was born, he attacked, stealing away my mother's soul to be imprisoned forever, cut off from the one thing she cherished above all others—freedom and peace. She's now his slave in the spirit world, trapped with no hope of ever being free."

"You're still free," Erin pointed out. "That must give your mother's spirit some comfort." Jacque shrugged. "Why hasn't your grandmother stopped her son now?" Erin asked.

"He's her only son," Jacque said. "Could you take the life of someone that you love?"

That gave Erin reason to pause. She wasn't sure. "I would have tried to do something."

Jacque's eyes turned to stone. "Bloodlines are a tricky thing. We cannot choose who we are tied to for better or for worse."

"Well, your father has come after one of my bloodlines, and I cannot simply let that slide. But he didn't do it unprompted." Jacque looked confused. "There is a dark family that my family has been fighting against for centuries. I believe that your father hunted my sister at their urging as a way to get to me." Erin chewed her lip. "If I can spare your father, then I will, but not at the expense of my sister."

Jacque studied Erin for a moment before reaching into her pocket, revealing a small red bundle. She held the bundle in her hands as if she was weighing her options. She closed her eyes and thrust the bundle towards Erin.

"There's nothing I can do to change my grandmother's mind," she said, still staring at the bundle. "She won't do anything that would end the life of a member of her bloodline. She made the mistake of waiting too long. I won't."

Strong protection magic came off the red bundle. Erin's startled face looked at Jacque with a renewed sense of confusion. She was almost certain that the red bundle hadn't come from Eulalie. Eulalie's magic felt old and strong. The magic coming off the bundle was strong but felt young and unsure.

"Your sister was the kindest soul I've ever met," Jacque said, looking Erin in the eye. "Everyone I know is afraid of me because of who my family is and what they've done. That's the reason why I don't do magic. But for your sister and her kindness, I will break my rule just this once. It's called a gris-gris and will protect you from my father's magic for a little while. It might give you more of a fighting chance."

Erin's eyes welled up. "Thank you," she whispered and clutched the gris-gris close to her chest. "I won't tell anyone where I got this."

Jacque swallowed, giving Erin a smallest of nods. "I appreciate it." She stood to leave but stopped, staring at the red bundle. She closed her eyes, and when she spoke again, her voice was full of emotion. "Don't waste precious moments trying to save him. Some people have lived in the dark for so long that it has become a part of them, and they cannot live outside it." She abruptly turned and walked out of the room, stopping just before she crossed the threshold. She looked back over her shoulder at Erin. "I hope you can save your sister before it's too late," she urged and then closed the door behind her.

Erin stared at the little red bundle in her hands for longer than she would have liked to admit. Jacque's selfless action filled her heart with hope for her people. She also understood just how much the little bundle would come to cost the young mechanic, so she should not waste it.

She lunged for the windows, vaulting over the couch. With a flick of her wrist, she closed the blinds, plunging her room into semi-darkness. She then dove for her duffle bag, pulling out a black bowl, a bundle of herbs bound together with twine, and a crystal pendulum. Erin scooped the items up, dashing about her hotel room, looking for the local map that she bought the moment she arrived in town. With all items at hand, she plopped on the couch, clearing the coffee table with a swipe of her arm. Magazines, books, and an empty glass tumbled carelessly to the floor.

She unfurled the map, laying it over the coffee table. Most of the corners hung over the edges of the table, but Erin didn't mind. The heart of the town and the local outlying areas were splayed out in front of her. She knew that her sister wasn't outside the town boundaries of Moonbay. The invisible bond that tethered her to her sister told her that much. Carefully, she laid out her tools before delving into the wellspring of her power.

Like always, Erin felt a surge of clarity and confidence when she touched the deepest portions of her magic. She gently called out to it, reaching for the strand that floated to her. When she grasped it, she felt the power pour into her body like water into a bowl. When her body could hold no more, she opened her eyes. Her room shimmered with light from the other world, lights flickering like the sun on water. Light and dark energies coexisted harmoniously. Erin wished that the rest of the world worked like that, but sadly, those who walked the two different paths of magic clashed against each other at every pass. Erin turned her mind back to the spell she needed to cast. She would have to cleanse the space of any unwanted energies, essentially making a magical clean room before she could work.

Erin closed her eyes once more, cupping her hands and furrowing her brow slightly. At first, nothing happened, but slowly, a spark of emerald light formed in her hands. The spark grew and grew until it was the size of a softball. It was then that Erin released it, watching it float to the northern portion of the room. Once the emerald ball of light was in place, she repeated the process creating a ball of yellow light to the east, then red at the south, and lastly blue to the west. The multicolored balls shimmered in their respective corners in the room, their lights taking over all others in the space.

Now, Erin spread her arms wide, and ropes of white light shot out from each orb, connecting one to the other. There was one more flash of light that caused her to close her eyes, and when she opened them again, the balls of light, white rope, and all other energies had disappeared, leaving only a clean presence in the room.

She lowered her arms and took several deep breaths, pulling the clean presence inside, letting it drive away any lingering doubts or darkness inside before she continued with her spell. Her eyes took on an otherworldly sheen, and the voice that came from her mouth is not her own. It echoed with the sound of a thousand other voices reaching out across the centuries in search of one of their own. Erin threw the bundle of herbs into the black blow. It ignited with a flash, burning quickly, sending a purple smoke into the air.

"What is hidden by the dark, come to the light. What is lost, be found. Part the vale, clear the shadows. Come forth into my sight."

Over and over, Erin chanted the words, her spell bolstered by the power of her ancestors. The tension in the room built. Wood crackled against the strain, and papers stirred in an unnatural wind. Her eyes glazed over as she stared into the smoke. As the tension in the room reached its zenith, an image took shape in the smoke.

It was a decrepit looking shack in an alcove along a swampy river. Dozens of small boats were docked along the base of the shack. Flickering lights shone out from the windows, creating the illusion of safety, but the image filled Erin with dread. Without taking her eyes off the image in the smoke, she reached for the pendulum, letting it swing freely in her grasp. She held it over the map and continued her chanting. At first, the pendulum circled the map lazily but quickly gained speed like a dog tracking a scent. Faster and faster it spun, making smaller circles with each rotation until, with a jerk, it stilled over a spot on the map.

Erin stopped chanting, letting the tension ease out of her and the room before she looked at where the pendulum landed. Slowly, everything returned to normal. She released her protection circle with a half a thought. The magic she called up sunk once more into its proper place, leaving Erin feeling slightly empty. She breathed a sigh of relief and looked at the map.

"Dark Horse Lake," she read. It seemed like a fitting place for a man who called himself the Dark King of the Bayou. She sucked on her teeth, slumping back into the couch. The lake was several miles outside of Moonbay, meaning she would need a boat to get there. She didn't want to involve an innocent civilian but knew better than to go without some sort of backup. She doubted if Eulalie would help her, and Jacque had already done what she was willing to do. That left Erin with only one person that she could reach out to for help, but she didn't like it.

SEVEN

WHAT WAS IT about police stations that made you feel guilty? Even Erin wasn't immune. Her knee bounced rapidly as she wrung her hands, watching the officers going to and fro from the corner of her eye. She mused that perhaps the reason why people feel so uneasy in police stations was that everyone had something that they were trying to hide, the proverbial skeleton in the closet. Well, Erin had come to expose a skeleton of her very own, and she hoped that it wouldn't land her behind bars or in a padded cell. She closed her eyes and sent a silent prayer to her ancestors that she would come out of this meeting unscathed.

And while she didn't remember much about the other night, she did distinctly remember Remy telling her that he had been brought up not only to believe in the supernatural world and its forces but also to have a healthy respect for it. She knew that she was taking a risk, but it was one that she had to make. Unbidden images of Caleb's face when he discovered she could do magic flashed before her eyes. His look of hurt and betrayal permanently etched into her mind, a warning against exactly what she was about to do, what she had no choice but to do.

"You really must stop falling for me," Remy teased as he walked up. Erin tensed. His tone came off more forced than flirtatious. His body posture was guarded and wary. Instantly, Erin's mind went to the worst-case scenarios. Was she too late? Had Sébastien already killed her sister—or worse?

Sensing her turmoil, Remy shifted into police mode. His posture relaxed, and he took a cautious half step forward. "What happened? Have you heard something? Did someone contact you?"

Realizing that his odd behavior was due to something else and not her sister's case, Erin shook her head, casting her dark thoughts aside. "No, no, I just needed to talk to you about something. Something that I think is crucial to finding my sister."

Remy crossed his arms, wary once more. "All right."

Erin looked around the busy police station furtively. "Can we talk in your office?"

Remy sighed heavily, pinching the bridge of his nose. "Sure." He turned and waved for her to follow. They wove their way through the other officers' desks until they reached one of the private offices in the back. The glass in the door was frosted with gilded lettering. Long windows ran along the length of the wall on either side of the door, but the blinds were drawn down. Remy held the door open for Erin, motioning for her to go in first.

Almost two years of stumbling into cleverly laid traps, Erin's first instinct was to scan the room physically and magically for any signs of danger. She had a gut feeling that she could trust the detective, but she had been wrong before. Cursing at herself, Erin swallowed her fear and doubt and looked at the room once more with clear eyes. What she saw surprised her and was at odds with what she knew of Remy.

His office was sparsely furnished, and much of what was there looked worn and handed down. She had expected the working equivalent of a man cave. Yet what she got was a man who didn't care about frivolous things but was deeply proud of his accomplishments. The wall directly across from the door boasted three windows that let in tons of natural light, softening the dark woods in the room. A small, heavily patched plain couch sat directly under the windows, with a pillow and a spare blanket carelessly thrown into a corner. Clearly, Remy had spent a night or two in his office. His desk was dark and classic, but the varnish was cracked and chipped in many spots, with numerous rings from coffee cups across its surface. Not a stray scrap of paper could be seen. Two straight back chairs that sat in front of the desk offered the only other sitting space in the room. A small, long bookshelf claimed the other side of the office, along with pictures from Remy's time before the force and during it—football games, holiday parties, and fishing trips. A bit of the knot in Erin's stomach loosened. If things went well, then she knew that she could count on the detective having her back.

Remy closed the door and strode across the room to take his seat behind his desk. Gone was the charming man she had shared drinks with, flirted with. The edge he carried the moment she walked through the door was only amplified by the privacy of his office. Erin wondered if she had said more than she meant to last night. "So, is it that you've come to tell me? Judging from your face, it isn't good."

Erin took one of the chairs. Panic and self-doubt flooded her body. Her stomach rolled. Her heart beat frantically in her chest as her face heated. She gripped the arms of the chair with such force that her knuckles turned right. Remy wasn't Caleb, but if he reacted the same way, then she would just have to face Sébastien on her own. Calm trickled down from the top of her head all the way to the tips of her toes. It was now or never—a leap of faith.

With a click, the door locked. Remy's head shot towards the door, confused. Next, the blinds closed, and the room went pitch black, far darker than it should have been with closed blinds. It was like all light had been banished from the room.

"What the hell," Remy cursed, pushing his chair back. Even though Erin, like Remy, was completely blinded in the darkness, she knew undoubtedly that he had reached for his gun.

Too late to turn back now. Erin clasped her hands together, calling softly on her magic. She wanted to earn Remy's trust, not scare him away. A soft, spring green light shone through her fingers, the only light in the room. She focused on what she was doing and not the stunned detective who slowly released the hold on his pistol's handgrip as he lowered himself into his chair. She didn't see the way his eyes widened or his slack-jawed expression. When she felt ready, she slowly raised her hands, pulling them apart. The green light, now the color of new leaves, hovered in the air, illuminating Remy. Erin flashed him a shy smile before snapping her fingers. The ball of light erupted into thousands of green-gold butterflies that fluttered about the space in some mad dance of light and shadow.

She watched the butterflies dance around the room with a small smile on her face before turning her attention back to Remy. Remy tore his eyes away from the butterflies swarming his office to the impossible woman sitting in front of him. He closed his mouth and coughed. "Impressive light show, but what does it have to do with your sister?" he said with false bravado.

Erin felt a tug at the corners of her mouth. "Actually, it does," she said with a chuckle. Remy lurched forward in his seat, leaning heavily onto his elbows.

"Tell me," he demanded, so she did.

From discovering her hidden ancestry to the finding of the Great Library, Erin told Remy everything. To his credit, he listened calmly, only interrupting when he needed clarification on a certain point. When she finished, the detective had slumped back into his chair, dumbstruck.

"That's some tale," he said.

Erin snorted. "You should try living it."

Remy ran a hand through his coppery hair. "So, let me make sure I'm on the same page here ... your family is locked into some magical feud, and you think that your sister was lured out to the bayous and taken as a means to get to you?"

"You get a gold star," Erin joked, nodding her head. "And I need your help getting her back."

"How can I help?" Remy asked, flabbergasted.

"After I subdue the people who took my sister, you can lock them up," Erin explained.

Remy raised a brow. "And just how am I supposed to keep them locked up once they regain their abilities?"

Erin pondered for a moment. "I can make you a charm to keep them in their cell. There's a woman in town, Charlotte. She runs a voodoo shop. She might be willing to work something more permanently out with you."

"Perhaps," Remy mused, rubbing his tired eyes. "I swore to protect and serve the people in this community; I guess that extends to those like you who can bend the very fabric of the world."

Erin snorted, reaching across the table and gave Remy a small reassuring pat on the arm. As one who stood in his position not too long ago, she felt bad for him. It's no easy thing having your world turned upside down.

After a pregnant pause, Remy lifted his head, eyes filled with grim determination. "So, what's your plan?"

Erin settled back into her chair. "I know where Laura's being held. We'll need a boat, obviously."

"Obviously," Remy agreed. A bit of his old self came to the surface. "And lucky for you, I just might have one that will suit our needs perfectly."

Erin nodded. "I'll meet you at the docks on Creek Street just before sunset."

Remy chuckled. "Best time to have a magic fight?"

Erin laughed. "Not really. I have to prepare the spells and potions that will help keep us alive long enough to get my sister and get out of there."

The teasing laughter in Remy's eyes died. He gave her a curt nod, indicating that he understood and would be there. Erin gave him a tight-lipped smile before seeing herself out. She had many stops to make to get all the supplies she required.

Back in her hotel room, Erin leaned against the door and breathed a sigh of relief. She let the bags she carried fall to the floor and left them there. The good thing about magic being an integral part of a culture is that it makes finding spell supplies ridiculously easy—as easy as buying a pie. She strode across the room and picked up the phone, dialing her mother's number.

"Hello," answered her mother.

"Hey, mom," Erin replied, breathless. She could feel her mother tense on the other end.

"You found her." It wasn't a question. A tidal wave of strong maternal emotions rolled over Erin.

"Yes, and I'm going after her tonight." Erin bit her thumb. "Could you conference call Gran? We need to talk."

In a matter of moments, the three women were on the line together. Erin filled in her mother and grandmother everything she learned and her plan. Her grandmother was surprised that Erin exposed her secret to Remy, but her mother agreed with her daughter's decision.

"We have to stop living like we live in two different worlds," Erin's mom said. "I understand why we have to remain a secret from the rest of the world, but it wouldn't hurt to bring it in a little more than we have been. If not, then we might forget what we're fighting to protect."

Erin felt a rush of pride for her mother. The three women talked for a few minutes longer, Erin going over her contingency plans should things not go her way.

Erin only felt a little bit better when she got off the phone with her mother and grandmother. Whatever happened tonight, she knew that she had done the best that she could and that there was someone who would take up her mantle and continue her family's legacy. She sighed. There was no more time to waste on fretting the "what ifs." She had potions and charms to make.

Every available space in the tiny kitchenette had been overrun with minuscule bottles, plants, crystals, and scraps of paper with hastily scrawled spells. The former all came from the ever-helpful Charlotte, who was more than eager to rid her beloved home of the dangerous creatures that lurked along the borders of her beloved town. The latter from the vast collection of the Grand Library and her family's personal spell book. Erin smiled, glad that she had wondered into Charlotte's shop that day. After so many days of living in the shadows, she relished every friend, ally, and moment in the light. Perhaps one day she would be able to completely live in the light. Her heart swelled with hope.

Brewing and crafting the potions and charms that could help her to save her sister was a long and tedious task. She found herself longing for Fae, her ever stalwart familiar. Leaving him behind to keep an eye on things back home made sense. It still did, but given the unfamiliarity of the terrain and her opponent, she felt unsteady without him by her side. This was the first time she would go into battle without him. Erin tried to quell the butterflies in her stomach. Fae wasn't here with her, whether she liked it or not, so she'd best get over it and forge ahead. She had to for her sister's sake.

The sky had just begun to change from a vibrant blue to a dusky pink when Erin strode down the weathered wooden dock. Her hands clutched the strap of the satchel slung across her body tightly, the only sign of her nerves. From the satchel, tiny clinks, reminiscent of bells, chimed with each step, she was armed to the teeth, metaphysically speaking. She doubted, hoped, that she wouldn't have to use all of the charms she made, but she figured it was better to be over prepared than under. She had never faced Sébastien before and had no idea what he was capable of. She only had second-hand knowledge of him, so she had to prepare for everything, and therein laid the problem—you can't prepare for what you don't know.

At the end of the dock, Remy stood ready, waiting for her in a small skiff. His face was grim as he watched her walk towards him as if he was still debating telling her to stay behind. "You know, normally I don't bring civilians with me on a job," he said matter-of-factly.

Erin squared her shoulders and looked the detective straight in the eye, letting some of her magic shine through. "Trust me, I'm not a civilian," she countered. Remy swallowed, unnerved by the light emanating from her eyes. He made a face and held his hand out to help her board the skiff.

"All right, where to?"

"Dark Horse Lake."

The engine on the skiff roared to life. Erin sat near the middle of the boat while Remy deftly steered the craft out of the bay and out into the open water. As the boat skimmed through the waters, the pair remained silent, each lost in their own thoughts. Remy continued to question everything he thought he had known about the world. His gaze fell to Erin more than once during their silent boat ride. To him, Erin was small and fragile-looking. She was the type of woman that made a man want to be a protector and a provider, and yet she could lay him out with a passing thought. He shook his head. *That just goes to show ya,* he thought, *you can't judge a book by its cover.* Erin, completely oblivious to Remy's attention, went over spells in her head and prayed to her ancestors, the universe, and whoever would listen that everything would work out and they all would make it out of this adventure unscathed.

Nightfall had nearly set when they reached the opening of the lake that would lead them to where Laura was being held. Remy slowed the skiff to a near halt, letting it drift along in the currents. "Here we are," he said. "Do you know the exact location, or are we just supposed to skim the shoreline?"

"It's along a river just off the main lake," Erin said, thinking back to her vision.

Remy frowned. "There are three rivers that flow into the lake; you gotta give me more than that."

Erin chewed her lip and reluctantly dug into her satchel. She didn't want to use any magic until they found the place. Any spells she cast ran the risk of detection, thus losing the element of surprise. But between a small risk being detected and wasting time, Erin would rather take the small risk. From her bag, she drew out an owl feather, gently blowing on it until it shone like a small star in the growing night. She heard a sharp intake of breath from behind her. Slightly embarrassed, Erin looked back, flashing a half smile at Remy. He flashed her one back and urged her to continue. Erin closed her eyes and focused on her sister. She thought about Laura's smile, her laughter, her lust for life until the glowing feather was filled with the essence of who Laura was to Erin. It was then that she released it and watched as it hovered in the space before the boat, waiting for the command that would finish the spell.

"Find her," she ordered, and the feather flew off into the night. Without needing an explanation, Remy followed after the streaking light, realizing that he could just get used to having magic in his life. They sped straight across the lake as night settled all around them. Soon, the only light came from the moon overhead, the feather, and the fireflies. As they glided across the black waters, Erin sensed something up ahead. Alarmed, she stood and slashed the air with her arm. The feather stopped, dulled and floated down to the water. It floated away, disappearing into the night. Remy slowed the skiff, resting his hand on the handgrip of his pistol.

"What is it?" he asked tensely, his voice barely above a whisper.

Erin narrowed her eyes, straining her senses both magical and physical. "I'm not sure. But I think we're coming up on the entrance to the river."

Remy nodded and urged the skiff forward at a slow pace. Erin grabbed a search beam and used its light to scan the shoreline for the opening to the river that should take them to her sister.

After a half an hour of searching, Erin spotted a large, gaping, black hole in the dense shoreline. "There," she exclaimed, pointing with the searchlight and her arm. Remy steered the boat towards the dark opening to the river. As they crossed the threshold from lake to river, a malevolent presence washed over them. Erin involuntarily shuttered and reached once more into her satchel. From it, she pulled out the small red gris-gris bundle that Jacque gave to her. "Here," she said, turning towards the detective, "this will protect you from their magic." She hung the bundle around his neck with a tight-lipped smile.

"What about you?"

"My magic protects me, plus I have my own." She extended her wrist and showed him the bronze bracelet that her grandmother had given her what seemed like a lifetime ago. It would offer her some form of protection, but she didn't know how long it would hold up against an unfamiliar style of magic.

"I have something for you too," Remy said, reaching into the storage compartment on the skiff. He pulled out two bulletproof vests, tossing the smaller of the two to Erin. She hefted the unfamiliar object in her hands with a questioning look. "They may use more than magic against us," he stated.

Erin blanched. She hadn't even considered non-magic forms of attack. She cursed her own carelessness silently as she strapped the vest around her body. It was heavier than she'd realized and hot. Already, she could feel sweat forming under the areas protected by the modern armor, but she was grateful to the detective for thinking logically.

They cruised along the river, going as slowly as they could without completely shutting off the engine. The deeper they went, the greater the sense of déjà vu Erin felt. She knew down to the very marrow in her bones that this was the very same river from her vision. Her heart sped up in anticipation of the battle to come.

She knew that she's not the only one thinking about what may come when they reached the shack. Tension rolled off Remy as he scanned the shoreline with a practiced eye, and once again, Erin was grateful for his presence. Not only did she feel better knowing he had her back, the way he reacted to her magical reveal had gone a long way towards healing the wounds still left over from Caleb's rejection. She hoped that one day Caleb might come to forgive her for keeping such an important part of who she was from him and apologize for the harsh words he said.

So wrapped in her thoughts, Erin didn't notice the small ransacked build come into view as they rounded the corner, but Remy did. He cut the engine and let their momentum and current carry them along silently towards the house. Unlike her vision, there were no boats docked along the edges of the shoreline and the small weather-beaten deck. The pitch-black windows appeared to draw in the surrounding, coming off more like gaping mouths than windows. But it was the silence that disturbed Erin the most. Not a bird, insect, or even the wake from the skiff made a sound. A shiver ran down her spine. The closer the skiff got to the shack, the more oppressive the air became. It pressed in on her as if it was trying to figure her out, find a weakness to exploit. Erin gritted her teeth, clutching her satchel tighter. She sent one last beseeching prayer to the universe for victory.

Remy docked the skiff without making a sound. Wordlessly, he leaped onto the dock, slowly removing his pistol from its holster. He motioned for Erin to remain where she was while he scouted the visible area for any potential threats. When he deemed it safe, he helped Erin out of the boat. The boards groaned slightly under her weight.

Remy pulled her close to him, leaning down to whisper into Erin's ear. "Magic or not, I'm the cop, so I'm going first. Stay behind me and stay alert."

Erin nodded, suddenly overcome with fear. This situation was vastly different than what she was used to. Most of her fights up to this had been pretty straightforward. But this time, there were too many unknowns. With one hand, she clutched the back of Remy's vest, her other hand hovering just inside her satchel, fully prepared to grab a vial or cast a spell. Where ever Remy stepped, Erin did. When he paused, so did she. The dock heading up to the house wasn't terribly long, but their overcautious approach made it feel a mile long.

After what felt like an eternity, they reached the rickety staircase, more of a ladder in truth, that led up to the house itself. Remy shot Erin a questioning look over his shoulder. She gave him a small nod, hoping that the fear she felt inside hadn't shown on her face. Remy went up first, using one hand while the other pointed his pistol at the door. When he reached the deck, he remained crouched and quietly walked up to the door while Erin waited at the base of the stairs. When no one came bursting out of the front door, he waved her up. Erin relinquished her death grip on the satchel, reaching for the railing of the stairs. Carefully, she placed her foot on the first step, testing its strength. Just because it hadn't given out under Remy didn't mean that it wouldn't give out under her. Step by step, she crept up the stairs, her eyes locked onto the black and vacant window ahead. She awkwardly tried to copy Remy's approach, but it felt clumsy and wrong.

Remy waved her towards him, silently urging her to put some pep in her step and get back into her position behind him. Erin complied, breathing a small sigh of relief. So far so good. She quietly dug around in her satchel, looking for the vial that would release a paralytic vapor when smashed. A blur of sudden movement caught her attention. Remy no longer crouched beside her. Roughly, he shoved Erin behind him before he shifted his weight to his back leg and, with the other, kicked the door in with a shower of dust and splinters. Erin stood where she was, open-jawed at this new development. Remy surged into the darkness beyond the threshold, pistol sighted in ready to fire.

Swearing, Erin scrambled after the detective, keeping a low profile as she saddled up to the nearest interior wall. It was far darker inside the house than it had any right to be. Breathing heavily, Erin could taste the magic in the air. It left a bitter taste in her mouth.

Without warning, a brilliant light flooded the small space. Erin cried out in pain as she shielded her eyes. The light faded just as quickly as it had arrived, but the damage was already done. Colorful dots danced across her vision whenever she blinked. Though she couldn't see her attackers, she could hear them chuckling at her. What happened to Remy? Was he all right? Was he dead? He hadn't screamed out when the light erupted. Eventually, her vision returned, and her heart sunk at the sight of Remy frozen on the spot. It didn't make any sense; the gris-gris she had placed around his neck should have protected him from any forms of magic. She scanned his frozen form for any signs of injury. It was then that she noticed that the red bag wasn't hanging around his neck. With a sinking suspicion, Erin reached into her bag, and sure enough, the first thing her fingers touched was the gris-gris. He had probably slipped it back into her bag when they put on the bulletproof vests. She silently cursed Remy and his idiotic need to protect her. Instead of yielding to her expertise, he left her outnumbered, with another person to protect. A chuckle brought her back to her current situation. She would berate Remy later, if they survived the night.

At the far end of the room, partially hidden by unnatural shadow, Erin made out six humanoid shapes that she prayed were people and not creatures she would have to battle. The shadows retreated, bringing Erin's opponents into the light. Four were undoubtedly followers of Sébastien. They smiled cruelly at Erin, their eyes alight with wicked glee. They flanked a man, who seemed to be made up of nothing but shadows. High immaculate cut black suit bled darkness, creating a dark aura around him. This was undoubtedly Sébastien Villére, the undisputed king of the bayou. He smiled at Erin, his impossibly white teeth stark against the midnight shade of his skin. Like his shadows, Sébastien's magical aura came off him in waves. With each crest of power, Erin's stomach clenched and rolled in rebellion in the face of pure evil. A small bit of movement forced Erin to tear her eyes away from her main opponent of the night to the last person in the room. This person was different. They were on their knees, bound and gagged on the floor, and the face was as familiar to Erin as her own—her sister Laura.

Erin's instincts screamed for her to sprint across the space and take her sister into her arms, to feel her heart beating inside her chest, to smell her skin, to feel her life force still coursing throughout her body. The five villains before her were the only reason why she showed any restraint. She knew down to her bones that if she did, then the battle would be lost before it ever began. Erin tore her eyes away from her sister, choosing to focus on the man responsible for her bondage instead. Cool fire filled Erin's veins as she slowly stood and squared her shoulders. She took a step forward, and then another. She positioned herself near Remy, offering him some semblance of protection. The time for being cautious had passed. Now it was time to fight.

"So you're the witchling I've heard so much about," Sébastien drawled, breaking the silence. His silvery voice filled the very air in the room. Erin could feel power laced through his words, urging her to lower her defenses and join him.

Erin snorted. She had encountered that trick before and by someone much stronger than Sébastien Villére.

"I didn't realize Connor had lackeys in the Deep South," Erin shot back, reaching into her bag once. Her hand wrapped around the first thing her fingers touched.

Sébastien laughed. "I am no man's *lackey*, little girl. We are partners, equals. He shares his wealth of knowledge and political backing, and I *let* him run his little schemes in my territory—for a small fee of course."

Erin snorted. "Whatever you have to tell yourself, but we both know who truly is top dog. Your usefulness will be gone once he finds someone more powerful, especially once I beat you."

"NO ONE IS MORE POWERFUL THAN I," snarled Sébastien. Though Erin kept her eyes locked onto Sébastien, she noted how his followers recoiled from his anger. Sensing a weakness, she pressed further.

"What about your mother?"

Sébastien's rage extinguished completely, and Erin saw his resolution quaver, but only for an instant; his cruel smirk returned.

"My mother keeps to her side of the world, and I keep to mine. We have our own laws here in the bayous. She will not interfere. We do not work against our own bloodlines."

Erin laughed. If only he knew that his own daughter, who had sworn to never use her magic, had made a gris-gris to protect Erin from him. Erin made a show of touching Remy with her other hand, seemingly searching for any signs of life with her other hand; hidden from Sébastien and his followers, she slipped the gris-gris into his pocket. Hopefully, it would keep him safe, if not reverse whatever spell held him.

Sébastien chuckled. "Don't worry your pretty little head over Detective Mercier. He's alive … for now. As an added bonus, he's fully aware of his surroundings. I wouldn't want him to miss the show."

"If you let my sister, me, and the detective go," Erin said, stepping in front of Remy, "we will leave you in peace."

Sébastien scoffed, "That yuppy warlock has put a pretty impressive price on your family's head. Everyone who follows the dark is hunting after you and yours. There will be no peace for you, and I intend on collecting the bounty. With it, I will finally be able to rise up and claim my rightful place in this town."

From the corner of her eye, Erin saw a muscle feather in Remy's jaw. Hope flared in her chest. Perhaps the gris-gris was working faster than she thought. She fought to keep her face neutral, although she did turn her face towards him. His eyes burned with such hatred, such anger that Erin's throat tightened. Even though the detective didn't have any magic at all, he was fighting the enchantment that held him captive. His will was stronger than the will of the person who cast the spell, and that was the key component of any spell— the strength of will. You didn't have to be stronger; you just had to be more stubborn.

Filled with a renewed sense of resolve, Erin shifted into a fighting stance. Her hand wrapped around a potion bottle, and she held it above her head. For a fleeting moment, her eyes drifted away from the man who sought to hurt her family for financial means and locked eyes with her sister. She was not surprised to see that her sister's eyes were not filled with fear but with anger and resolve. Laura cut her eyes to the side quickly. Erin cast a protection circle around herself and Remy to distract the others from her other actions. Her sister cut her eyes again towards the only shelf that ran along the entire western wall of the tiny space. Erin shifted her eyes to the shelf. It was filled with various bones, bleached white with age, unfamiliar plants, crystals, and glass vials. One vial caught Erin's attention. While the other vials were empty, this one contained a silver whip of smoke that shone with a soft white light. Something about it seemed familiar to her. It was just like the light her ancestors had when they came to the physical plain! There was a spirit trapped in that vial, and Erin had a gut-wrenching idea on just who it might be.

Jacque had said that her mother's spirit had been trapped by her father, the man standing so near to her sister. If Erin found a way to free Jacque's mother, maybe she would seek revenge on the man who ended her life and imprisoned her. Or she could disappear. Or she could go on a murderous rampage. It was a gamble but one Erin was willing to take since the odds weren't exactly stacked in her favor.

Emboldened, Erin hurled the vial in her hand at her enemies' feet. As it shattered against the floor, she shouted an archaic word. The four followers of Sébastien were thrown into the back wall. Erin cut her eyes to the shelf. Everything rattled; several things fell and broke—but not the vial that held Jacque mother's spirit.

Erin's had caused Sébastien to stumble but had not thrown him back. Laura had been completely unaffected because the spell would only affect dark magic users. Sébastien snarled at Erin, pulling a knife from behind his back. The blade of the knife was no ordinary blade. It was darker than the deepest pits of hell, and it seemed to draw in all the light around it. Erin froze at the sight of it, causing Sébastien to smile cruelly before he yanked Laura's head back, bringing the evil blade down towards her exposed throat.

EIGHT

ERIN SCREAMED. Her magic erupted from her like water released from a dam, filling the too small space. Wood groaned under the pressure. Candles flared to life, burning through the wax almost instantaneously. Time slowed to a near stop as the blade neared Laura's pale throat. Laura's eyes were closed and seemed to be uttering a prayer—or a spell.

Magic's nature may be to twist the very fabric of the world, but it is the world's nature to snap back once into place. Time regained its normal flow, leaving Erin to watch in horror as the malevolent blade neared her sister's throat.

She yelled again, sending another raw, unfocused wave of power out, shattering all the glass in the room. She fell to her knees, exhausted and barely holding on to consciousness. Never before had she done something like that in the physical world. She gulped air greedily, trying to stave off the encroaching darkness that had crept into the borders of her vision.

The world took a collective breath, and the point of the blade pressed against Laura's throat, drawing a single drop of ruby. Then the whole world went to shit.

The vial containing Jacque mother's spirit fell to the floor, releasing her spirit at long last, erupting into a whirlwind of silvery smoke that dissipated momentarily thereafter. Remy stumbled forward, free from the enchantment that held him captive. It only took him a breath to recover, pulling the trigger of his pistol, firing a bullet into Sébastien. A wall of blue light erupted from Laura that mingled with Erin's magic that still simmered in the air around them. The sisters' energies blended into one another, creating a force that shattered the few remaining windows and ripped the flimsy tin roof off the tiny house. Thousands of stars sparkled in the night's sky overhead while the soft droning of the cicadas filled the empty space.

Sébastien was thrown back by the gunshot and by the power unleashed by the sisters. He landed a foot away from Laura, clutching his shoulder. From beneath his hand, a crimson stain spread to encompass his entire shoulder. Seeing that her sister had not died under the enemy's blade, Erin breathed a sigh of relief, calmed the wild magic she had released in desperation. The bonds around Laura's wrists and ankles burned to ash, freeing her. Laura gulped for air and crawled towards Erin with tears in her eyes, weak from her own spell. Erin let out a laugh that was mixed with a sob, reaching out for her sister.

The moment her sister's hand clasped hers, Erin pulled her sister in for a tight embrace, her arms wrapping protectively around Laura. The two sisters sobbed into one another's hair, clinging to the other as if they were the other's lifeline. Remy smiled at the sisters, positioning his body to shield them from Sébastien, who still lay bleeding on the shack's floor ahead of them.

Now, it's my turn, rasped a voice through the silence that had settled in the aftermath of destruction and chaos.

Every head snapped towards the western wall where a willowy woman took shape. The woman bore a striking resemblance to the mechanic who had been moved to go against tradition to help the two sisters, though she was made up of silvery smoke and shadows, not flesh and blood. However, there was one striking difference between the specter and her daughter. The specter's eyes blazed the very fires of hell itself as she gazed at the man she once loved enough to share a life with, to make a child with. Her lovely face contorted into the stuff of nightmares, her mouth elongating, revealing impossibly long, sharp teeth. Her fingers morphed into claws perfect for mangling the flesh of the living. The woman grew in height, her bones becoming more prominent and elongated until it looked nothing like a woman at all but a monster that would have fit right in with demons from hell. Sébastien drew breath for a scream that he never got to utter. The demon disappeared from beneath the ruined shelf to reappear directly in front of the man who had caused her so much pain, so much suffering for the past twenty years. Faster than anyone could track, she latched onto her former husband's throat, hoisting him into the air.

His feet swung freely in the air as he fought against the monster that he created with his lust for power and control. Gasping, he tried to fight against her, but his hands went right through her body. He tried to shout spells at the terrifying specter but was silenced by a swift and brutal squeeze that left him wheezing.

Erin, Laura, and Remy watched the terrifying scene unfolding before them with equal expressions of horror painted on their faces. But there was nothing they could do. Even if they wanted to help him, they couldn't. Jacque's mother would take her revenge out on them as well as her former lover.

Remy pointed his gun toward the ghost that was strangling the life out of her former husband as he gently pushed the sisters towards the shattered doorway. Erin steered her sister in front of her, eager to get her to safety first.

"Don't leave me," Sébastien pleaded over the gruesome shoulder of Jacque's mother.

Erin turned and faced the man who would have gladly killed her and her sister for a profit, and she found herself feeling pity for the man. Gone was the arrogance, the cruelty, the hunger. The only thing left was fear. Fear of dying, fear of pain, fear of facing the great beyond. But even though she felt pity for him, that didn't erase all the evil he had committed. Remy gently tugged on her arm.

"We're not done here," she said, turning toward him. "Take my sister to the skiff and wait for me. If I'm not back in five minutes, take her and leave."

"No!" Laura cried, latching onto the shattered doorframe. "We're stronger together. You need me."

Erin shook her head and gently clasped her sister on the shoulder. "I need to see this through to the end, but if something goes wrong, you need to make it out of here so you can take up my mantel. I name you as my heir." Erin lovingly stroked her sister's hair. "You are the future. You have a great heart, and that's what the world needs—both worlds.

Laura stared at her sister with tears in her eyes. Remy gave Erin a tight-lipped smile before steering Laura away, leaving Erin alone with a demon and its soon-to-be victim.

"Please help me," Sébastien pleaded, extending his bloodied hand out to her. Erin tried to not focus on the blood dripping from his outstretched fingers.

"How many of your victims begged for the same thing?" She crossed her arms. Here was her hardest trail, her test to see if she truly had what it took to be a Guardian.

She had to push her emotions aside to be judge and jury and to take that final step towards assuming her role entirely.

"But I am in the mind to spare you," she said, "only if you give up the dark and strive to walk in the light. Besides, I don't think your daughter Jacque would want her mother to become a killer over you." Jacque's mother's spirit lost some of its sharpness at the mention of her daughter. She looked to Erin with such a painful hunger in her eyes that reminded Erin of her own mother when Laura went missing.

Some of his former cruelty leached back into Sébastien's eyes as he let out a chuckle that turned into a wet cough. Erin saw a thin line of blood eek out from the corner of his mouth. "Oh, she's already a killer. She's been killin' for me since the day I ripped the soul from her body and sealed it in that jar."

"Only because you made her," Erin countered, clenching her fist. "She left you when she realized just how far gone in the dark you were. She didn't want that type of life for herself or for Jacque."

Jacqueline, said the demonic specter. Erin tried to not flinch when its bright burning eyes turned on her.

"She is a fine woman," Erin told the specter. "She is fierce and independent, determined to not be as callous as her grandmother and father."

The specter began to glow and lose her terrifying form. When she once again looked like the human she had been in life, she smiled. "Can you do something for me, Guardian?"

"Anything."

"Tell Jacque; tell my daughter that I am sorry I wasn't able to be around for her. Tell her that while I revile the crimes her father committed, I do not regret meeting him because that was the only way she would have been born. Tell her she has been my shining light in the dark, my only salvation in this world."

Erin's throat tightened, and her eyes burned. "I will."

Sébastien struggled against the ghost of Jacque's mother once more, drawing her attention back to him. "This is not your arena, Guardian," she said to Erin, not taking her eyes off her former husband. "You have no right to pass judgment here. But I do."

Erin bowed to the spirit, realizing the truth in her words. Sébastien's struggles turned frantic as Erin took a step backward towards the exit.

She began to recite the death prayer that had appeared in her book the day before she left. "May your spirit go swiftly into the beyond. Pass through the cauldron without looking back and be cleansed. May your spirit find its place in the lands of your ancestors. May you find peace there. So mote it be."

Jacque's mother bowed to Erin and released Sébastien's throat. He fell to the floor with a thud, rubbing his throat and gasping for air. Shakily, he got to his feet, drawing both breath and power, but it was no use. Jacque mother's eyes flashed brightly once more as she hurtled through Sébastien's body. When she appeared on the other side, she was not alone.

The spirit of Sébastien stared in horror as he watched his own body slump to the floor, lifeless. Jacque's mother kept her grip on him as she turned to face Erin. "I knew that he needed to be stopped long before I ran away. I waited too long, and it cost me dearly. Do not wait too long to deal with your dark one."

Erin didn't ask how she knew about her war with Connor. She assured Jacque's mother that she wouldn't with a small nod and turned her back on the two ghosts. She kept her eyes forward and fought the urge to glance over her shoulder as Sébastien began to scream. She knew that what was happening to him was not for the living to see.

Outside, she could see Remy fighting to keep Laura in the skiff. The tenacious young woman threatened the detective in such a way that impressed her older sister. When Laura saw Erin standing on the small deck, she sagged against Remy with relief.

Erin made her way down to the skiff, deliberately choosing not to answer Remy's silent question about what happened in the hut. With a huff, Remy started the engine. It flared to life with a roar that made both Erin and Laura flinch. They settled near the middle, clinging to the other tightly. Remy steered the skiff out towards the lake and back towards town.

From the corner of her eye, Erin saw Laura raise her face into the wind. She kept her eyes closed, and the wind whipped her hair back. A small smile splayed across her lips as if the wind was cleansing her soul of all the darkness from her time in captivity. Erin felt herself smile like her sister.

The wind roared in her ears, nearly drowning out the roar of the engine. Serenity poured into her, easing the tension in her body and calming the frantic thoughts in her mind. She slowly released her death grip on Laura and looked over her shoulder to Remy at the helm. He stared intently ahead until he sensed Erin's gaze. Their eyes met, and she mouthed "thank you." He flashed a half smile before returning his attention to navigating the dark terrain around them.

No matter how peaceful the return trip was, Erin didn't truly relax until the skiff had been safely docked under the brilliant lights of Moonbay Harbor. Laura still clung to Erin, as the full weight of her ordeal settled onto her young shoulders. Remy gave the pair a look that caused a sickening feeling in the pit of Erin's stomach.

"What?"

Remy pressed his lips together. "There's no easy way to explain all of this."

"Don't worry about it," Erin assured the detective. "We have plenty of practice explaining the unexplainable."

Remy shook his head and reached for his phone. "For some reason, I don't doubt that." And with that, he called into the police station. A short police cruiser ride later, Erin and Laura found themselves sitting in the police chief's office, spinning their lie to half the police force.

"So, let me get this straight," the police chief said, pinching the bridge of his nose. "You were taken by a group of people who weren't happy that you and your college friends were rebuilding the old fishin' camps along the bayous?"

Laura nodded her head. "I guess they didn't want anyone to mess with their stash houses or whatever."

The chief narrowed his eyes. "But you can't tell me just how many there were or their names?"

"No sir," Laura lied. "They kept me knocked out most of the time. The only name I can give you is Sébastien Villére. I heard that one a lot."

A ripple of excitement went through the listening officers. Laura pushed on.

"They wanted to hold me hostage until they found a way to halt the construction altogether. I think they were going to kidnap more volunteers."

The chief turned his shrewd eyes on Erin. "And just where do you come into all this, Miss McManin?"

Erin gave her sister a small squeeze. "I had come to town a few days ago after hearing that my sister had disappeared. I asked everyone I came across if they had anything on my sister's disappearance, and Detective Mercier can contest to that."

The police chief didn't look to Remy who stood just behind the sisters. His eyes bored into Erin's as if he was attempting to compel her to tell the truth. There was no way that was going to happen, so Erin continued with her carefully crafted story.

"Mr. Villére sent a message to me, stating that he wanted to discuss a ransom for my sister."

"And why didn't you come to the police with this bit of information?"

Erin tilted her head, acting confused. "I did, sir. As soon as I received the message, I contacted Detective Mercier. I asked him to accompany me."

This time, the chief did look at Remy, but not in any way that would be conceived as good.

"I didn't tell him the whole truth, though," Erin interjected, lying quickly. "I told him that there was a possible lead on my sister and wanted him to come with me."

"It wasn't long before I realized something was up," Remy interjected. "I recognized the area as the suspected hideout for Villére's seedier enterprises. But by then, we were out of cell range. I decided to carry on because if Ms. McManin failed to show up, I feared that harm would happen to her sister."

Remy's answer seemed to placate the police chief— barely.

"When we arrived at the predetermined location, I made Ms. McManin remain in the skiff while I investigated. It was then that I discovered a young woman gagged and bound on the floor. That was enough for me to enter the building, but when I did, I discovered that Mr. Villére lay dead on the floor."

The four followers hadn't been found at the scene when the forensics team found the small shack where Laura had been held. Erin suspected they woke; saw their leader dead and fled. If they were smart, they would lay low until things settled down. Erin wanted to remain and finish them off, but this was not her territory. These were not her people, and though she wanted to help them, they would have to handle it on their own.

"Yes," the police chief said, grabbing a file folder. "The M.E. thinks that Mr. Villére suffered a heart attack." He raised a questioning brow at Remy who shrugged in return. The police chief sighed, leaning back in his chair, and studied the two women seated across from him.

Erin felt a bead of sweat run down her spine. Their story made sense. Sure, it had some holes, but none big enough that would let the chief detain them further. But the longer they picked at those holes, the bigger they would get. Giving Laura a mental nudge, they combined their powers and sent it out amongst the officers. The only person they left untouched was Remy. The sisters erased any critical thoughts or nagging concerns the officers had. They pressed the acceptability of their story and urged them to let them go.

The chief's shoulders slumped. "I may not fully understand all that has conspired here today, but I'm glad that we were able to rescue your sister before anything irreversible happened." He sighed heavily, studying the sisters one last time. "Take care in the future."

Laura sagged with relief while Erin thanked the chief and the entire police department for their efforts. She steered her sister out of the building and into another waiting police cruiser. Thankfully, the streets were empty when the cruiser arrived at Erin's hotel.

"We'll be keeping an eye on you ladies until you leave," the officer who drove them said. "Just want to make sure no one shows up after you."

Erin thanked the officer with a tight smile and ushered her sister upstairs to her room. The first thing the sisters had to do before they took a well-deserved sleep was to call their mother. This, of course, meant another round of tears and telling what happened, although this time it was the truth. With multiple promises to keep themselves safe and to leave as soon as they could, the sisters hung up the phone.

Laura fell back onto the bed, groaning. "I really, really, really want a long, hot bath"

Erin pointed towards the bathroom. "Have at it. I'll be back in a little bit."

Her sister shot up, pink sparks snapping through her hair. "What?"

"I promised Jacque mother's spirit that I would relay a message to her."

"What about the police guard outside. They'll follow you, and they'll want to know why you're visiting the daughter of the man who kidnapped me."

Erin smirked. "That's what magic's for."

Most of the lights in the apartment building were out. Only a few shone bright, determined to keep the night at bay. Erin stared up at one such light, wondering if the person inside usually was up this late or couldn't sleep. This was not going to be a pleasant visit either way, so Erin squared her shoulders and walked up three flights of stairs and knocked on the door.

Jacque answered the door, seemingly unsurprised to see Erin standing on her doorstep. "So it's done, then." Erin couldn't get a read on the other woman's emotions. "I'm making a drink. You want one?" Jacque left her door open, leaving the choice to Erin whether or not to walk through.

Jacque's apartment was surprisingly feminine for someone who worked in a predominately male and extremely dirty profession. The colors in the apartment made Erin think of a sunrise over the water. The furniture did not match, yet all went together somehow. It was a welcoming home. Erin rounded the corner to see Jacque sitting at a small, white, two-person table. In front of the vacant seat rested an empty glass, and right in the middle sat a fifth of whiskey. Jacque had already poured a glass for herself.

Erin joined her and poured a glass of her own. She gulped half of it down, letting the burn clear her head. She had no idea how the other woman would react to the message from her long dead mother.

"I didn't kill your father," Erin whispered.

Jacque raised a brow. "A cop came to my door an hour ago and told me that my father's dead."

"I know, but it wasn't me who killed him."

Jacque cocked her head as Erin took a deep breath before plunging into the night's story for the third time. Through it all, Jacque sat quietly. Not once did she interrupt Erin. The only emotion she showed was when Erin relayed her mother's final words. She swallowed and looked off to the side. Erin stopped to let her regain her composure before continuing. She remained silent after Erin finished her tale. Erin waited for a minute before rising from her seat.

"I am sorry about your mother and father." Again, no reaction from Jacque. "Thanks for the drink." Erin quietly let herself out, locking the door behind her. The nearly full moon low in the night sky. If she didn't hurry back, dawn would come before she got any sleep at all. Her thoughts kept going back to the young mechanic and what her life would be like now. Her father had killed and imprisoned her mother for twenty years, forcing her to do his dirty work. When her mother finally earned her freedom, the first thing she did was to kill her father. Erin sent a small prayer to her ancestors, asking them to watch over Jacqueline and keep her safe. She hoped that the young woman would one day find peace and acceptance, although Erin highly doubted it.

"You know I am more than capable of taking care of myself, Detective," Laura quipped from her position on the bed. The detective had his feet propped up on the coffee table, flipping through the channels on television. "Especially in my sister's room with all her magical protections."

Remy chuckled. "That may be true, sweetheart, but Sébastien's people aren't exactly known for their forgiving nature, and not all of them will come at you with magic."

Unable to argue the point, Laura huffed, slouching back against the pillows. For two days, Erin and Laura lingered in Moonbay. They stayed partially to let the former recover from her ordeal and partially because the police hadn't cleared them to leave the state yet. And after two days of confinement, Laura had started to get cabin fever. Thankfully, Remy had incredibly thick skin and gave it back to the young woman just as easily as he took it.

Laura stuck her tongue out at the detective's back before curling back up with her magazine. A knock at the door caused both to tense. "Open up," Erin called out from the other side. Laura let out a breath and resettled. Remy opened the door and took some of the bags Erin carried.

"Thank you," she exhaled, shifting the rest of the bags around. "I thought I was going to lose both my arms there for a second." She flashed a bright smile before meandering her way towards the kitchenette.

"What's all this for?" Remy asked, holding a can of diced tomatoes.

"We're having a celebration!"

"Oh," Laura said, uncurling her limbs to join the others in the kitchenette.

Erin nodded, her smile growing larger. "I just got back from talking to the DA, and we're cleared to go back home!" Laura cheered and flung herself over the counter, throwing her arms around her sister's neck. "He said that they are still investigating your kidnapping, but for now, there's no reason for us to linger. He did say that if they arrest the others responsible, he would like you to come back and testify."

"Do you think they'll catch them?" Unease flashed in Laura's eyes.

Erin opened her mouth to answer, but Remy beat her to it. "I *will* catch them." Laura searched his face for any signs of insincerity or falsehoods. Finding none, the worry faded from her face, allowing her internal sunshine to come through again.

"I had hoped to make an authentic Creole meal tonight," Erin said, changing the topic.

Remy looked at the food she bought and made a face. "Oh no, chér, this is not how you have an authentic Creole supper."

Erin frowned at her purchases. "What do you mean? I bought all the ingredients."

Remy scoffed at the canned goods. "Real food, good food, has to be made from scratch. That's what my mom always said, and it has never failed me yet." He threw the groceries back into the bags. "We'll drop these off at a soup kitchen along the way to the fresh market. Then it's off to my place."

The sisters exchanged a look. "So you're a chief as well as a knight in shining armour," Laura teased with her hands on her hips.

Remy gave her an over-the-top bow, flashing his cockiest grin. "At your service, my lady." The trio laughed and carried the bags down to Remy's car.

Remy's house was in a quaint neighborhood only a few miles from the fresh market. The street lights were already on by the time they arrived. Nearly all the houses had lights on, providing quick flashes of the families inside. Erin drank in the peace and serenity around her. Remy's house was distinctly male, but it still gave off an impression of welcome and warmth.

Soon the air was filled with the tantalizing aroma of spices and the sizzling of meats. All three were congregated in the kitchen, laughing over story after story. Erin couldn't have thought of a better way to spend their last night in Moonbay.

Everyone turned at the sound of someone knocking at the front door. Laura and Remy looked to one another, confused, and then to Erin—who was already headed towards the door.

"I hope you don't mind," she called out over her shoulder, "but I invited someone else to dinner."

Laura squealed in delight when she spotted Jacque on the other side of the door. Jacque's usual serious demeanor softened at the sight of Laura, and the two embraced each other tightly before Laura dragged her off to the kitchen. Erin shook her head over her sister's antics and turned to welcome the second person in.

"Young people," Charlotte joked, pulling Erin in for a quick hug. The middle-aged woman beamed up at Erin, as proud as any mother. "I brought Hummingbird cake. Can't have a dinna' without dessert."

The good thing about some meals is that there is no way to make them in small amounts, which was a good thing for the five people now seated around the table, sharing a meal together. Erin couldn't keep the smile off her face as she looked out over the table. Remy and Charlotte were already elbow-deep discussing how they were going to bring the wayward magical members of their community to heal. Jacque hadn't taken her eyes off of Laura from the moment she arrived. Almost as if she was afraid that if she were to look away, then Laura would disappear forever. Laura talked animatedly, her eyes bright with hope for the future. Even though Laura had almost lost her life, she still intended to make her life in Moonbay once she graduated. Erin wished her sister the best.

By dessert, most of the conversations had died down, everyone filled to the brim with good food and good company. Lara, Jacque, and Remy chattered away in the kitchen as they cleaned up, while Charlotte dug books out of her purse for Remy to read later. Erin tied the top of a trash bag closed and carried it out to the bin.

The night air was cool and sweet, and Erin couldn't help but pause and breathe it in. She was ready to go home, but she would miss this place.

"It is a nice night," said a voice behind her.

Erin dropped the trash bag and spun around, magic flaring to life at the tips of her fingers. If one of Sébastien's followers wanted to seek retribution, they would regret it. In the pale light, Eulalie stood calmly, hands folded in front of her.

"Pardon me," Erin said, dousing her magic. She remained wary of the other woman and waited for her to speak, but she never did. "Jacque's here. Would you like to come in for a drink? Something to eat?"

Eulalie shook her head. "I don't want to ruin my granddaughter's evening." The older woman looked towards the house and sighed sadly. "Ever since Jacque was little, she carried this shadow in her soul. It's probably the reason why she won't use the gifts she was born with. Her way of making penance for a crime she didn't commit." Another sigh. "But now, that shadow has lifted, and she is at peace. She still refuses to accept her gifts but is at peace." She turned her amber eyes onto Erin. "This is because of you and your sister, which leaves me in your debt."

From the look on her face, Erin safely assumed that Eulalie was not happy about it. Eulalie continued to stare at Erin, perhaps in hopes that the younger woman would tell her that there was no debt between them. Too bad for her, because Erin had no such intentions. Eulalie allowed her son to run wild and unchecked, causing imaginable levels of suffering. As far as Erin was concerned, the older woman was just as guilty, not to mention that she was still pissed that she put her under a spell. If Eulalie was about to offer Erin something that could help her win her fight against Connor, she would take it.

Eulalie pursed her lips and thrust a small wooden charm at Erin. She gave Erin the smallest of nods before turning and disappearing into the night.

"Good night to you too," Erin muttered into the dark before returning to the party.

All Erin wanted to do was fall asleep. She and her sister had to be on the road first thing in the morning if they were going to make their flight back home. She would have already fallen asleep, but her sister was apparently having a hard time getting settled. Erin stifled a groan and turned over.

"Spit it out already."

Laura rolled over to face her sister. "Sorry. I guess I got a lot on my mind."

"You wanna talk about it?"

"I guess," Laura mused, chewing her cheek. "How did you know that Dorshire was the place for you? The place where you belonged?"

Erin mulled over the question carefully before she answered. "I can't really put it into words, but there's this feeling." She waved her hand over her chest. "Almost as if your heartbeat is in tune with the beat of the land. Your breath is similar to the wind." She bit her lip, struggling over the words. "I heard music. I heard the song of the land, and it moved me. I knew the song was for me, and that I was a part of it." She shook her head. "That doesn't make any sense; I'm sorry."

"No, you're right," Laura assured her. "I feel that way about this place. I don't want leave, but I don't want the magical side of my life to be my only life." Erin nodded her head. She struggled with the very same thing.

"I wouldn't worry too much about it right now. You got plenty of time. Finish college, hone your magical skills and figure out what type of person you want to be. But whatever you choose, I know you'll be great at it. You're *my* sister after all."

Laura smiled and rolled over. "God! Erin, go to sleep, or we won't get up on time."

Erin made a face and hit her sister with her pillow. Her sister let out a mock squeal of shock, curling up into a little ball. Still laughing at her sister, Erin resettled and fell asleep at last with a smile on her face.

NINE

COMING HOME MEANT several things for Erin. First and foremost, she couldn't truly relax until both she and her sister were once again protected by ancestral magic. Unfortunately, that also meant that they had to dodge the swarm of reporters who were determined to get the scoop on her sister's disappearance. It was only thanks to her mother that the vultures didn't dare venture beyond the gate. Once Laura crossed the threshold, everyone broke down into tears again. Jessica held her daughters in close, taking comfort from the beat of their hearts and the scent of their skin. Her children were home safe and sound at last. Even Erin's father embraced the two young women, and when he pulled away, Erin could have sworn that there were tears in his eyes. Her anger towards her father eased ever so slightly. He couldn't help his nature any more than she could. Perhaps it was time to cut the man a bit of slack.

It took every ounce of restraint for Erin to not jump right back onto the first plane heading to Ireland. She knew that the longer she waited gave her enemy more time to prepare against her. But she also understood that her family needed this small measure of happiness before things went to hell again. And this time, it would be all or nothing.

All that day, Jessica doted on her daughters as if by her sheer will, she could chase away the darkness they had endured. The two sisters let their mother do this, knowing it was the far easier alternative. Elise praised the girls over their endeavors, but underneath her praise, Erin sensed a hint of worry. Her grandmother knew that the battle wasn't over and seemed to sense what Erin had planned.

That evening, after her father had retired for the night, Erin called the rest of her family down into the kitchen. They each took a seat around the informal dining table, each face serious and waiting. Now, Erin and Laura filled in their mother and grandmother on the truth of what conspired in the bayous of Louisiana.

Rage simmered in Jessica's eyes when she learned about the bounty placed on her family's head. Elise didn't seem all that surprised. She once more praised the girls for their quick thinking and skill.

"But what next?" demanded Jessica. "First, that bastard nearly kills my daughter just so he could chase her to the other side of the world just so he could get his hands on our book. Then he sends children, *children*, after Erin, hoping to either turn her or kill her. *Then* he kidnaps my youngest and places a price on our heads—dead or alive. What are we going to do?"

Elise folded her fingers under her chin. "There are stronger protections we can place around ourselves and those we love. Of course, we could always seek out those who may be sympatric to our situation and offer assistance."

"Everyone has their own problems," Laura countered. "We can't ask them to shoulder ours as well. Plus, we're supposed to be the ones that *they* call on for help, not the other way around."

Their mother shook her head. "It's too much for one person, one family to handle. Things need to change."

"Change doesn't happen overnight," Elise pointed out. "We have to start somewhere."

The conversation around the table turned from theory to tactical applications. Elise offered one spell after another, but they were too advanced for Erin, Laura, and their mother, and Elise lacked the power to perform them. On and on they went, talking in circles, ever searching but never finding the solution. Erin got up from the table and headed straight to the liquor cabinet. She grabbed a bottle and four glasses before returning to where her family was still locked into a heated debate over how to resolve their conflict.

"There's only one way to resolve it," Erin said, pouring a shot. "We have to take Connor and his family out once and for all to end this war before more innocent people get hurt."

Her mother, sister, and grandmother stared at Erin in disbelief. There is a brief moment of silence before they all start to speak at once.

"He's too strong," cried her mother.

"You haven't finished your training," her grandmother pointed out.

Her sister, though, was on her side. "Let's go! That creep had me kidnapped. I'm game."

Jessica and Elise continued to strongly object while Laura argued the point. Their voices grew louder and louder, threatening to wake up the only member of the family not in on the secret war. Erin raised her hand for silence. She was mildly surprised when her family respected it and fell silent. She explained her reasoning to them, not as a daughter, granddaughter, and sister, but as the head of their clan.

"We could train and study for a lifetime and *still* not be equal to Connor. That's just the plain simple truth. He has had a lifetime to hone his ruthlessness and skill." Elise looked down at her lap, ashamed. Erin reached across the table for her grandmother's hand. She gave Erin a slight smile before taking Erin's hand. Erin gave it a squeeze, letting her grandmother know that she bore her no ill will for running away from the war and keeping them ignorant of their magical heritage.

"But that doesn't necessarily mean that we're at a disadvantage." Her family gave her confused looks. "Because we weren't brought up in the same environment means that we don't have the same limitations that he does.

Evil or not, Connor still plays by the old rules. *We* don't have to. We don't have the same social trappings ingrained into us like he does. We can still surprise him."

"Like we did on Halloween," Laura interjected. Erin acknowledged her sister's point with a dip of her head.

"Exactly."

Jessica furrowed her brow. "We can't count on that anymore. You've pulled one too many surprising victories for him to continue to underestimate you. Don't you underestimate him."

Erin shrugged. "Perhaps, but I'm tired of running, tired of reacting. I'm tired of spending half my time looking over my shoulder, waiting for the next attack. It's time we take the fight to him and end it once and for all. That doesn't mean that we don't still need to prepare, but this time, we are going into this fight ready ... or as ready as we can be. It's time to end this."

She sat back and let the others mull over her words. No matter their decision, she still had every intention of meeting Connor in the field of battle, but she would feel better if her family stood by her side.

Her sister was the first to speak. "I am with you, Erin, no matter what happens." Erin flashed her sister a grateful smile and slid the bottle to her. Laura grabbed a glass and poured a shot. She threw it back, setting the glass back down with a bang before sliding the bottle to their mother.

Jessica held the bottle with both hands, staring at it without seeing it. "I'm terrified," she admitted, closing her eyes. When she opened them again, they were filled with resolution. "But my family has been attacked one too many times. It *has* to end." She poured a small shot and threw it back, shuttering. The bottle slid to Elise.

Elise looked at the women seated around the table. Though outwardly she is calm, inside there is a swell of pride for her family. Here they sit, ready to run headlong towards the threat instead of running away like she did. Elise said nothing but poured a shot all the same. She sipped at it and slid the bottle back to Erin who smiled at them all.

Erin poured one last shot and raised it into the air. "For the family."

"For the family," the other's echoed.

Erin tipped the glass back, swallowing. The sound the glass made when it hit the table echoed louder than it had any right to be, echoing throughout the silent house. The choice had been made; they were no longer running. Now it was time to arm up and face the dark shadow that had been allowed for too long to walk the earth.

The bayous of Louisiana undoubtedly had their beauty, but nothing could beat the unassuming charm of Dorshire. Erin's spirit soared at the sight of the brownstone buildings lining a quiet street. Her heart beat faster knowing that just beyond the sleepy town, green hills rolled as far as the eye could see. Her bones hummed with each step as the land sang its special song just for her. No, there was nothing better than coming home. She rambled along the sidewalk, relishing each step on her home turf. She felt surer of herself than she had in days. It made her feel drunk.

Although she'd rather be at home hugging her familiar Fae tightly to her chest as she filled him in on everything, there was something that Erin needed to do first. She stopped at the entrance of a store, taking comfort in its familiar decor and presence. The plants in the shop window had changed, but nothing else had. A small bell jingled merrily as she pushed open the door. A well-known, comforting voice called out from somewhere beyond the mini jungle carefully maintained inside.

"Erin!" Moira cried, holding her arms out wide when she came around the corner. "I grew so worried when I hadn't heard anything. Is your sister all right? What happened? How's your gran and everyone else? Come now; I'll put on the tea."

Laughing, Erin steered Moira towards the back office to fill her in. By the end, Moira sat in utter silence.

"What are you going to do now, dear?"

"It's time to take the fight to him," Erin said, resolute.

Moira reached out to grasp Erin's hand. "Is there anything I can do?"

Erin took Moira's hand and gave it a firm squeeze. She knew that what she was about to ask would put the other woman in more danger than she already was. But Connor had come after her too, and if he won, then there would be no one to protect her or the rest of the village. "Yes."

A large, two-story home loomed ahead in the glow of Erin's headlights. Ivy clung to most of the exterior walls, reaching as high as the second floor in some places. Twin chimneys framed either end of the house, smokeless and cold. Near the front door, a pair of eyes gleamed in the dark. Erin smiled. Of course, her familiar Fae would be waiting on the doorstep for her. He sat stoic until Erin closed the truck door. Yowling, he scampered to his mistress, leaving glowing footprints in his wake. Laughing, Erin knelt and accepted her familiar with open arms. She held Fae tight to her chest, tears running freely down her face while his purring rumbled against her chest.

"Welcome home, Mistress," Fae greeted.

"It's good to be home, my friend," she said. "We have much to talk about."

Fae ceased purring, regarding his mistress with solemn eyes. "Aye, that we do."

Kim groaned, rubbing her face. The next semester was due to start in two weeks, and she *still* had a ton of summer work to complete. She would have been further along, but for some reason, there had been an influx of folk witches seeking sanctuary for their spells. With Erin still off in the states, searching for her sister, that left only herself and Orrin to handle it all, and he was the only Librarian. She just helped out when she could. Cursing evil teachers who delighted in giving their students work during holidays, Kim returned back to her work. She was so absorbed that she failed to notice the doorway that appeared on the wall behind her.

Erin smiled when she saw her young student hunched over one of the many mahogany desks in the Grand Library. She drew in the comforting scents of old books, ancient wood, with just the faintest hint of smoke from lanterns or candles. Fae strode towards the young empath on silent pads. He rubbed against her legs, startling her.

"Fae!" Kim exclaimed, nearly jumping out of her seat. It was then that she saw Erin smiling at her from the new doorway. Without a word, Kim flung herself at her mentor. "You're all right! You're all right! I knew you would be!"

"What in the blue bloody blazes is going on down there?" Orrin appeared from the depths of the library to peer over the edge of the railing. The furrows on his face smoothed at the sight of the young redhead hugging Erin. "Welcome back."

"It's good to be back," Erin shot back. "Do you two have a moment? We have some things to discuss."

Orrin frowned and motioned for Erin to wait a moment. Kim stepped back, instantly chewing on the strings of her hoodie. And once again, Erin filled in her friends on what transpired in Louisiana and what her plan was going forward. Though her outward demeanor was calm, inwardly, she was becoming weary. She was tired of telling the same story over and over again. She was tired of the same arguments for why she should keep her head down. All she wanted to do was get started and see the end of her long and useless war. But this time, Orrin and Kim took everything in without a single complaint.

"I'll do what you ask," Orrin said. "I think that it's the only way you'll pull through this alive."

"Wow, Orrin," Kim quipped, "thanks so much for the vote of confidence."

The corner of Erin's mouth twitched. "It's all right, Kim. I know he's right, and before you ask, no. You are too young to get involved in all this."

The teenager opened her mouth to argue but stopped. She crossed her arms, slumping back into her chair. She knew she wouldn't be able to chance either of the adults' mind, and secretly she was relieved. Her gifts were passive and would be no use in an all-out drag-down fight.

With nothing more to say, Erin left. She had one last stop to make, and this one was the most dangerous of them all.

Just like that day, so long ago it might as well be a lifetime, Erin flinched at the overbearing pressure of darkness and despair that hung over the property belonging to Connor and his ilk. Squaring her shoulders, she took a step onto the driveway. Instantly, her senses reeled. Her vision and stomach rolled against unseen forces. Her bones ached under immense pressure. Her muscles turned to jelly, quivering with each agonizing step, but she didn't stop. She needed to draw out the occupants of the castle ahead, and this was the only way she knew how.

Lights flared to life in the castle. The rumble of an engine filled the air. Erin stopped her agonizing trek up the driveway and waited for the silver car to make its way to her.

The car stopped a few feet shy of Erin, but with the headlights shining directly into her eyes, she couldn't see just who was driving. Two doors opened and closed. Two sets of footsteps crunched against the gravel. Two shadowy shapes blocked out the light.

"To what do I owe *this* pleasure?" Connor drawled, leaning against his car. He looked exactly the same as the last time Erin saw him. She vividly remembered the look on his face when her spell sent him flying out of her parents' house. The corner of her mouth twitched at the memory and gave her the courage to say what she needed to say.

"How was your flight?" Erin smirked. Connor frowned, gray fire danced along his fingers. She hid her surprise at the small display of magic. Never before had he ever allowed his magic to be seen. Had she finally gotten to him, or was it a show to intimidate her?

"You must want something to come all this way and to subjugate yourself to this torture," Connor said, reigning in his frustration. "You know, there *are* easier ways to contact me. Have you heard of this marvelous device called a cell phone?"

Erin forced a smile onto her face. "Yes, but this is more satisfying."

Connor smirked. "If you want me, all you have to do is ask."

Erin blanched. "Don't make me sick. We have unfinished business, you and I." Connor raised his brow. "It's time we end this. I know you're tired of it just like me."

A feral grin blossomed on Connor's face. "Did something happen to *push* you in this direction?" Erin remained silent, knowing full well he was just trying to get a rise out of her. When she failed to respond, Xander shifted nervously beside Connor. He stilled when his cousin shot him a nasty glare.

"Very well," Connor agreed. His tone suggested that the whole ordeal was a minor inconvenience and not the compellation of centuries of fighting between the two families. "In accordance with our traditions and laws, then?"

"In accordance with our traditions and laws," Erin agreed. "By the next full moon, I will meet you in the astral plane, and we can settle the score once and for all."

Connor pondered her words, no doubt searching them for any signs of entrapment. Erin wondered if he would refuse or give a counter offer. But he didn't. Without a word, Connor returned to his car, kicking up dirt and rocks at Erin as he turned around and sped back to his castle.

Erin lowered the arm she raised to shield her eyes, silently cursing Connor. She was covered in dirt and slightly bruised from some of the gravel flung her way, but none of that could erase the sly smile blossoming on her face. *Just you wait, you son of a bitch*, Erin swore, *I will make you pay for every sin you've committed and then some.*

She turned to make the agonizing trek back to her truck when an icy wind blew along her spine. She froze as the wind crept up her spin to caress her face. "When this is all over, *bitch*," Connor's voice said into her ear, "I will dance on your family's grave and tear down everything you've built."

Erin cried out as a sharp pain flared on her cheek. Her hand pressed up against the hurt reflectively. When she pulled it down, a thin line of blood stained her hand. Eyes blazing, she faced the castle and made a rude gesture. As she got into her truck, she could have sworn that she heard malicious laughter ringing out into the night.

Laugh while you can, Erin thought, gripping her steering wheel tightly, *but I* will *win this fight.*

TEN

ONE MONTH. Erin only had one month to prepare for a battle against the greatest foe she would ever hope to meet. One month to prepare for a battle that her ancestors had seen centuries ago. A battle they spent their lives and the lives of their children and their children's children readying for. She hoped that all their suffering and sacrifice would not be in vain. She hoped that she was strong enough, smart enough, to see this fight through to the bitter end. But if she wasn't, well, best not think about that just yet.

Days ticked by, the silent countdown to either her salvation or her demise. She tried to not dwell on the potential for failure for too long. They would weaken her just as sure as a physical blow, and she needed to be in peak physical form.

During the day, Erin carried out her life like normal. She went to work. The start of the summer semester was a welcome distraction. She used lesson plans and essays as a wall against the questioning portion of her consciousness. She went for Sunday dinners with Moira's family and met her friends down at the pub for a drink to remind herself of all that she fought for, all that she held dear to her heart. She bought books and spent any downtime she could carve out, curled up in her favorite chair and got lost in new and exciting worlds to save what was left of her sanity. But her nights ... her nights were vastly different.

At night, she lived in a world that mortals would never witness, a land of shadows and mists, nose deep in long forgotten and ancient texts, gleaming new spells and rituals from their dusty pages. With each new spell, she laid down layer upon layer of spell and enchantments. Nearly every inch of her territory had been carved up with half-finished spells, ready to be unleashed with a simple stroke or half a thought. Erin spent her nights readying for war.

Erin stood in a barren landscape covered with cool mists that swirled around her ankles. She was as incandescent as the sun, a brilliant source of green-gold light in the half-darkness around her. Fae added to Erin's light with his own vibrant shade of green. They stood transfixed on the seemingly impenetrable forest before them. Erin breathed slow, steady breaths; the glittering light around her pulsated with each breath. The unseen ground beneath her feet began to rumble as a stone wall slowly rose up from the mists. Sweat beaded along Erin's brow and down her back. She clenched her teeth as she strained against the effort to raise the wall higher.

When the pressure of the spell became too much for her to bear, Erin lowered her arms, releasing the spell. She wavered on unsteady feet, gasping for air. Fae leaped from Erin's shoulder to inspect the wall while she centered herself. He walked along the length of the wall, sniffing and prodding it with his paw. Whatever he gleaned from the wall seemed to please him. He turned and trotted back to Erin, with his tail high.

Erin, however, scowled at the wall. "It's only three feet," she complained. "I could hop over that; no problem."

"If this was in the physical world. ye could," Fae said, sitting at her feet. "But it's not. Ye must remember that things on this plane are not always like they appear."

Erin stared at the wall, still doubtful. "Go on, then," Fae urged. "Go and see if ye can 'hop' over it."

Erin made a face at Fae before walking over to the sad little wall she spent so much of her energy on to bring into existence. The wall looked even less impressive up close. Barely three feet high, it appeared to be made of river stones, with black mortar holding it all together. Erin shot another questioning look over her shoulder. Fae urged her on with a wave of his paw. Exhaling through her nose, Erin went to put her hand on top of the low wall, only to find that she couldn't. Her fingers met an invisible barrier, and no matter how hard she pushed against it, her hand would not pass through. Eyes wide, she spun around to face a particularly smug-looking Fae.

"Still think ye can hop over it, Mistress?"

Erin stuck her tongue out and waved for her familiar to follow her. She pressed her hand against the invisible wall once more, this time turning the magical locks that would allow her and Fae to pass through. The invisible barrier gave way, allowing Erin's hand to pass through. Power danced along her skin, prickling like a thousand little insects. The sensation continued up her arm as more went through. Erin quickly pulled her arm out. She turned her hand over, wiggling her fingers; they were unmarked and unharmed. She pushed her hand through the barrier once more, and the rest of her followed.

Bright sunlight warmed her face. Erin blinked against the light, turning to look at the thick woods behind her. A smile broke out across her face. Not only did the wall protect and mark her boundaries, but it also served as a shortcut to the heart of her territory in the astral plane. She turned and trotted after Fae—who was already halfway up the dirt path that led to the cabin in the middle of the clearing. The cabin itself hadn't changed much in the year Erin created it, but the same could not be said for the rest of the clearing.

To the left of the cabin stood a stable. In it, Erin housed the sendings, humanoid creatures made up of shadows and night she created to help protect the boundaries of her territory. She had spent two weeks straight making them, almost non-stop. The ten sendings she created shuffled in their stalls, eager to be put to the task they were created for. Erin would release them when the time was right. She didn't want them to waste away before the final confrontation with Connor.

Originally, the cabin had been made up of wooden logs, but now it was made of impressive stone bricks. There were other changes as well. Some Erin made herself, and some Fae had made to help his mistress train. A circular patch of barren earth now claimed the area where the fire pit used to be. Black lines ran the perimeter of the circle and flowed inward to create archaic patterns. This was where Erin and Fae practiced the fighting spells and techniques she would possibly use.

The more she worked within the space she carved out for herself, the more it became in tune to her needs, especially the cabin. Rooms would appear and disappear as needed. Books or scraps of spells were found in the oddest of places; Erin's favorite so far was the spell for sendings that revealed itself amongst the shards of a cup that she had knocked off. So, when Erin walked into the cabin and noticed a new, strange-looking door in what used to be a wall, she wasn't concerned in the slightest.

"Fae, did you add a new room?" she asked, studying the door. Fae used his own unique form of magic to bolster the defenses when Erin was otherwise occupied.

Fae shook his head. Erin groaned, both curious and apprehensive over what the cabin's newest addition would be. Sometimes the new rooms had dark ambiances like dungeons or chambers of a similar ilk. She suspected that some of her more vicious ancestors made unsolicited contributions to her preparations. And if the door to the new room was any indication, she might have to destroy the new room like the others.

The door looked like it would not be out of place in some medieval castle with its thick, rough wood braced with iron bands. The handle to the door was nothing more than a giant metal ring. Tentatively, Erin approached the door. Fae trotted between her feet, sniffing at the base of the door.

"I wondered when this would show up," he mused, sitting back on his haunches. "I was about to suggest it to ye if it didn't show up soon on its own."

Erin cocked her head. "What's beyond this door?"

Fae turned his head and looked at his mistress over his shoulder. Though he couldn't smile, Erin could have sworn she felt a smirk in his words. "It's the armory, Mistress. Did ye think ye'd head into battle with no weapons?"

Curiosity peaked; Erin took hold of the metal ring and gave it a tug. The door swung open easily and soundlessly. Erin paused in the threshold, uncertain. Fae had no such reservations. He shot through Erin's legs, yowling for her to get a move on. Erin shook her head and followed him.

The medieval theme continued inside with floor-to-ceiling stonework. Great wooden beams divided up the walls and supported the ceiling. The walls to her immediate left and right were filled with empty weapons racks.

"For an armory, there appears to be a startling lack of weapons," Erin commented dryly as she ran her hand over the racks as she walked further into the armory.

Fae chuckled and continued down the hall. Erin studied the racks, mildly intrigued. Some of the racks were clearly meant for swords, spears, and the like, but others were clearly for more modern means of combat like guns and possibly heavy artillery. She shook her head, wondering if magic would ever stop surprising her.

The racks gave way to a large space that opened up to the outside. Erin speculated that it was an old-fashioned smithy. Several large work tables took up most of the open space. What was left had been taken up by a forge whose flames already burned white hot and the anvil that sat to the right of it. Scattered around the anvil were other components vital to the creation of metal objects.

A cool breeze filtered in from the open space behind the forge. When Erin looked around it, she was surprised to see the stables in the distance. The cabin had added the armory and smithy *after* she walked in or the room wasn't visible from the outside, either option was entirely possible.

Erin stood in the middle of the space just in front of the anvil. Slowly she turned, taking in everything. She had been preparing for weeks for her final confrontation with Connor, but with the arrival of the armory and the smithy, the reality of the situation came crashing down on her. She was actually about to engage in a full-on war for the lives of her family and the land. Her heart started to pound heavily in her chest as fear and doubt gained a foothold in her mind. She gazed about the room wide-eyed and slightly panicky until she saw a small t-shaped stand in a far corner of the room. She chose to focus on that rather than her encroaching panic.

"What's that?" she asked, pointing.

Fae followed her finger, seeing what she saw. "That's where yer armor will go when yer not wearing it."

"And just how am I supposed to make all this stuff?" Erin asked, waving her hands at the empty racks and armor stand, panic giving her voice a sharp edge to it. "In case you haven't noticed, I'm not exactly a blacksmith."

Fae leaped up onto the anvil and started to wash himself. "Ye don't have to be," he calmly mentioned. "If yer done bleating like a lamb before the slaughter, I'd be 'appy to tell ya how to use this space." He turned his brilliant green eyes on Erin and stared at her with the full force of his fairy power.

Guilt washed over Erin. Fae was right. She was allowing her emotions to get the better of her—again. She needed to keep a level head, or all would be lost. Erin closed her eyes and took several calming breaths. She didn't attempt to quell the panic threatening to rise inside and take over. She instead took it and channeled it into something that was more constructive—how to create her weapons and her armor.

"Tell me."

Fae's otherworldly light dimmed to be replaced with pride. "Ye must call out to yer allies. Command them to send ye a boon. When they send it, cast it upon the fire, and it will transform. The stronger the ally, the stronger the item will be."

"Can I make it into anything, or will it just happen?"

Fae shrugged. "It depends on the boon. Sometimes an ally will send it with a specific function in mind, but more times than not, it is left up to the one who called."

Erin ran her hands through her hair, filled with wonder and hope. A treacherous thought blossomed, making her chest constrict. "Fae, what if I call and no one sends anything?"

Her familiar's eyes flashed a brilliant green. "They must. Or they will answer to me and my kin. The rules governing alliances is as old as the world itself and cannot be broken lightly." Erin felt her chest ease. "Even Connor, as dark and twisted as he is, has to follow the traditions."

Erin let the issue go. Fae knew more about the inner workings of the magical world, and if he felt that Connor would obey the laws and traditions of that world, then she would have to believe him—at least a little bit. Erin looked about the armory once more, this time with an eye on the potential. Her eyes landed on the T-bar that was meant to house her armor and frowned. She didn't have that many allies, and some of the ones she did have, she wasn't sure if they could be fully trusted. She chewed her bottom lip when an idea popped into her mind.

"Fae, could I use some of my family's relics to create armor and weaponry?"

The familiar scratched behind his ear while he thought about it. "I fail to see why not. Just remember, once ye use the relic, it's gone forever. There's no way to undo the transformation, so choose wisely. And I wouldn't suggest ye not call in on yer allies. Some might take it as an insult."

Erin nodded, seeing the wisdom of Fae's words. She would have to choose her relics carefully. Perhaps she should appeal to her ancestors to see what they would recommend. As Erin turned to leave the armory, she spotted a slip of paper with an ink pen sitting on top. She rolled her eyes and picked the items up. Clearly, the cabin wanted her to get a move on.

Standing in front of the forge, Erin contemplated the people she was about to call upon to assist her in her upcoming battle that would not only affect her but their lives as well. Erin scrawled the first name quickly, tearing it into a slip and casting it into the fire. The flames flared higher as they ate the tiny scrap of paper. Tiny flecks of green danced amongst the flames before flying up the flute and out into the world. Erin knew beyond a shadow of a doubt that Ylanna of the Gypsies would be willing to help her. Tapping her pen against her lip, she thought carefully about the next names on her list.

The Fairmont family. They no longer had any magic, but when they submitted their family's history to the Grand library, had offered to help in any way that they could.

Mary and Josephine, two hedge witches from the North Country; both were older than they looked but fiercer than anyone Erin had ever met. They were one of the first to forgive her grandmother for running and reaffirmed their allegiance to Erin's family. They loved to spoil Fae whenever they popped in for a visit, and he returned the sentiment.

Mark, a gifted healer from England. He had been visiting when he learned about the Grand Library's reemergence and offered his allegiance to help protect such a wealth of history and knowledge.

Those names were easy enough to offer up to the flames, but the next ones caused waves of guilt and apprehension to roll through Erin's already queasy stomach.

Orrin and Kim.

Charlotte.

The first two were very near and dear to Erin. The first was her first friend in this strange new world, and the latter in all actuality should have been left out of the fight. Erin only added Kim's name because she represented the future of the magical world, much like Laura, and therefore deserved as much of a chance to fight for it as anyone else.

Charlotte, on the other hand, Erin barely knew. The voodoo practitioner had no reason to involve herself in a centuries-long war halfway across the world. But Erin hoped that Charlotte would remember that Erin helped rid her home of its dark practitioner and extend Erin the same courtesy.

Erin wrote one last name but did not throw it into the flames like all the others.

Eulalie.

Erin debated the merits of calling in the favor that the old witch owed her. She didn't care much for the voodoo priestess. The few times they interacted hadn't left her with a warm and fuzzy feeling. But she couldn't afford to be too picky. With a resigned sigh, Erin vehemently threw the name in the flames. The flames rose one last time, sending green sparks into the air.

The call to arms complete, Erin brushed the ashes from the forge off her hands. She would have to wait and see what her allies sent her. With nothing left to do in the astral plane, Erin closed her eyes and focused on her tether to the physical world. From somewhere within her core, she felt a slight tug. She followed that tug back to the real world.

Erin sat still for a few moments, letting her soul resettle back into her body before getting up. She learned early on that if she tried to move too soon, her body felt alien, and more often than not, she would find herself on the floor. Firmly resettled, Erin opened her eyes and set off to her bedroom where the chest that held all her family's heirlooms sat. She would have to carefully select the pieces she would sacrifice to make her armor. While she trusted her allies, mostly to send her good material for weaponry, she could not in good conscience trust her bodily safety to them. That was a job for her bloodline.

Erin sat on her bedroom floor near the opened chest; rings, bracelets, pendants, necklaces, and all other kinds of jewelry littered the floor around her, and yet she was still no closer to choosing the relics for her armor. After consulting with Fae, they agreed that she would only really need five relics to forge her armor. But seeing the horde around her, she wasn't sure where to begin. A ghostly wind that carried a faint aroma of baked goods and soil caressed her cheek. Erin leaned into it, drawing comfort from the familiar touch. She was not alone.

"Hey, great-grandma."

Erin closed her eyes, laying her hands on her lap, and opened her mind up to the energies around her. In her mind's eye, she saw that her room was packed with the silvery forms of her ancestors. She gave them a slight bow before turning to the task at hand.

"The time has come at last," Kieran said, drifting into the forefront of the group. Erin bowed to the origin of her bloodline, and she could have sworn that Kieran had given her a small, proud smile in return. Erin wasn't sure because when she lifted her head, her formidable ancestor's face was back to its usual stony expression.

Clara, Erin's great-grandmother, came forward next. "No matter what happens, love, know that we are with you always. I cannot even begin to tell you how proud I am of you. You have suffered and yet have always remained open to those around you. You see the evils and wrongs in our world and set yourself against them—exactly like a Guardian should."

Erin bowed her head, beaming over the praise. "Thank you, all of you." She lifted her head and beheld the entirety of her family. "I would be lying if I said that I wasn't afraid."

"You would be a fool not to be," said one of the males. "During the times of The Trials, we all lived in constant fear of being found. We used that fear to keep our senses sharp. It made us think before we acted." He stretched out his hand over the relics scattered about the floor. "Use your fear to keep you sharp. Do not let it use you."

A small ring began to glow. Erin reverently reached out to take it. The ring was warm in her hand, pulsing like a heart. The ring was simplistic, something that wouldn't have drawn any attention outwardly, but in the inside of the band, Erin felt a small engraving. Upon inspection, she saw a rune that she was familiar with: algiz, the rune for protection. Erin smiled and set the ring aside.

This time, two specters came forward, twins. "You care for your family deeply," they said in unison. "You also pull in those around you. What ties a family together is not blood but the bonds we forge with them. We are all connected by these bonds in the web of life. Always nurture those bonds." In unison, they, too, extended their hands. Two different bracelets, one silver, and the other gold, glowed. The designs engraved on the bracelets were different from each other, and yet they went together. Erin set them next to the ring.

The next ancestor to step forward stunned Erin. She was a small child, barely twelve. The impossibly young matron gave Erin a knowing smile. "Times change," she said in way of explaining. "Age does not always mean that you're capable of completing what is required of you. You've always seen the true potential of the people who are drawn to you because of what you are. You open your arms wide, accepting all." The girl bowed to Erin. "Rule with wisdom and kindness." Erin opened her mouth to argue, but the girl had already faded back into the congregation, leaving a glowing circlet in her wake. Erin took it up reluctantly. She didn't want to rule. She just wanted everyone, herself included, to be allowed to live in peace.

Kieran and Clara stepped forward together. Erin instinctively straightened her spine.

The pair appeared to be having a silent conversation. Erin's palms began to sweat, but she remained silent. They would speak in their own time and not a moment before that. After what felt like an eternity but in actuality was most likely only a few short moments, they turned to face Erin. It was Kieran who spoke first.

"When I first had the vision, I knew that I had to act. My friends and teachers did not understand. I could not discern the time when this powerful enemy would land on our shores. They urged me to wait, to try and pierce the veil of time more to gain the full understanding. But I didn't listen. I understood that waiting was not the right path." Kieran tipped her head towards Erin. "In that, you and I are the same. Waiting is not always the best path. Sometimes you have to act and see what the fates have decided." Kieran stepped back, allowing Clara to come forward.

"I wish that you did have to be the one to bear this," she told Erin. "I wish that I had been bolder in my time, like you and your sister." She reached out to cup Erin's cheek. Erin closed her eyes, leaning into the calming essence of her great-grandmother. "Never lose that boldness," Clara urged Erin. "Always strive to act when you can. But remember that it's not always your responsibility to act. Let others be bold. Let others find their fire when it's their time to."

Erin bowed her head, acknowledging all the bits of wisdom her ancestors had bestowed upon her. The last item to glow was a small ceremonial dagger. Erin wrapped her fingers around it, bringing it to her chest. She looked out at the sea of shimmering people who loved her and wanted her to succeed.

"Thank you for all your help. It is an honor to be counted amongst you. No matter what happens, whether this is the end of our line or not, our actions will echo throughout time. It will be known that we stood up against the darkness and gave every last ounce of ourselves to protect those who could not fight for themselves. I can think of no better way to have my life remembered." The previous heads of her family bowed to her, bestowing their blessings. Erin bowed back, and when she straightened, the corner of her mouth pulled back into a smirk. "Although, I'd rather win."

That earned a chuckled from the ghostly congregation. Erin gripped the dagger tighter, silently promising to do her best with a small nod of her head. One by one, her ancestors vanished back to their places in the astral plane. Clara was the last to fade, blowing Erin a kiss before fading away, leaving Erin alone with Fae. Erin set the dagger amongst the other relics and gathered her familiar into her arms. He purred loudly, nuzzling his head under Erin's chin. He had no words to offer her; he didn't need them. His love for Erin came through loud and clear. Silently, Erin released Fae and then put the remaining relics back into the chest. She sealed it so that only a member of her family could open it. Connor would never get his hands on her family's heirlooms. Erin gathered the other relics and set them on the nightstand next to her bed. Night had fallen, and she found herself struggling to keep her eyes open. Kicking off her shoes and pants, Erin crawled into bed. Fae's eyes flashed green, locking the doors. Erin smiled as he curled up next to her on the pillow and was out a breath later.

Erin stood in front of the forge, palms sweating and slightly nauseous. Terrified of making a mistake that could result in the end of her life, Erin couldn't bring herself to throw the first relic into the flames. Once she did, there was no going back. Fae perched off to the side on a post, irritatingly silent. He would not tell her what to do; she had to make the first move. Erin closed her eyes and breathed in deeply. Her nerves calmed. She took in another and another until she felt as calm and still as a pool of water. It was time for the point of no return. Erin reached out and grabbed the first relic to be sacrificed for her armor.

She hadn't paid much attention to the design the other night when her ancestors helped her select the pieces, but now she did. The circlet resembled silvery branches woven around one another. Impossibly tiny leaves sprouted from the branches. Erin marveled at the immaculate details in something so small. She felt a twinge of regret over destroying something so beautiful, but she had no choice. She tossed the circlet into the flames before she could further second-guess herself. The moment the circlet landed into the coals, it erupted into a blinding white light. Erin squinted against the light and the heat, focusing on what she wanted the item to turn into. She didn't waste any of her energy worrying over making the piece pretty. She'd rather have plain armor than flimsy pretty armor. When the light dimmed, Erin removed the relic using tongs. It no longer resembled a delicate silver circlet. It was a shapeless, molten glob. The glob steamed slightly when it was placed on the anvil. Erin quickly grabbed a nearby hammer and struck the glob with all her might.

Clang. Clang. Clang.

Again and again, she struck the glob, keeping in mind what she wanted to create. When the glob resembled a crude helmet, Erin used the tongs again to pick it up and put it into the cooling trough. Steam billowed around her, bringing sweat across her brow. The helmet still steamed when Erin removed it from the trough. She set it on a small stone table so it could completely cool.

Erin turned to take a sip of cool water. Her shoulder and arm already screamed in pain. Her hand shook as it wrapped around the cup. She already felt a little unsteady on her feet. She wondered if she had the strength to finish her armor in one go like she had planned.

"Want to take a look at yer handy work, Mistress?"

Erin rolled her eyes at Fae, wiping the sweat from her brow. Erin gasped when she saw her helmet sitting on the table.

What sat on the table was something beyond Erin's skill to create. The helmet was a work of art that gleamed brighter than any star in the night sky. Erin walked over to the table. Her hand stretched out of its own accord, yet she was hesitant to touch the breathtaking piece of armor. Gently, she lifted it up, surprised by its weightlessness. She ran her fingers along the edges that bore hints of interwoven branches of a tree. These branches sloped gracefully away from the helmet, creating small points that would frame Erin's face. In those points, emeralds more vibrant than any she had ever seen sparkled in the pale light. Even the back of the helmet was ornate with leaves and flowers etched onto it.

"It's beautiful," Erin whispered.

She placed it on the armor stand and dashed back to the forge, eager to finish her armor. The ring was the next artifact to be cast into the flames. Like before, the ring erupted into a brilliant light. The ring melted away, leaving a molten glob larger than the original material could have provided. Erin repeated the hammering process. With each stroke of her hammer, the glob grew larger and larger. By the end, it took two tongs for Erin to transport the glowing armor to the cooling trough. While it cooled, Erin slumped against one of the pillars that supported the roof of the forge, savoring the cool breeze that whisked across her glistening forehead.

"Ye need to slow down," Fae commented from his post. "If ye continue like ye are, ye will surely faint or dip into yer life force."

Erin cracked open an eye. "Tap into my life force?"

Fae nodded solemnly. "Aye. It can happen when a witch tries to use more power than what they have. Everything in this world has limits, even magic."

Erin listened to her familiar's warning, filing it away for the future. She would research it more when it was all over, if she survived the fight. But bearing Fae's warning in mind, Erin decided to call it a day. When she stood back up, her world rolled, and darkness crept along the edges of her vision. It was a struggle for her to remove her new piece of armor, an impossibly light full set of chainmail, from the cooling trough, but she did. Her face broke out in a tired but proud smile as she added it to the armor rack.

Erin waved for Fae. He left the post he had been sitting on and leaped into Erin's arms. She felt a small surge of energy, aid from her familiar. It gave her the strength to leave the astral plane and return to the living world.

All the aches and pains from the astral plane were multiplied tenfold in the real world. Erin gasped, dropping Fae because her arms felt like lead and shook slightly. She took one unsteady step forward and nearly pitched onto the floor. The only thing that saved her from painfully face-planting was the edge of the sofa. She clung to that like a half-drowned sailor to a piece of driftwood.

"Oh!" was all that Erin got out before she completely lost her grip on consciousness. Fae yowled and nudged his mistress with his cold wet nose, but Erin didn't stir. Fae sighed and shook his head. *Young witches*, he thought, *they never learn*. A quick jump landed Fae on top of the couch. He took the corner of a throw blanket into his mouth and, with much grunting and huffing, pulled it off the back of the couch and over his unconscious mistress.

It was dark by the time Erin regained consciousness. She woke with a groan and pushed herself up on still shaky limbs. "What the fuck," she groaned. "Fae!"

Glad to see yer not dead yet. Fae sauntered into the living room with a bemused look on his feline face. Erin glared at her familiar. "I made ye some supper."

That startled Erin. "You can cook?"

Fae laughed. *Of course.* He then turn around to head back to the kitchen where, indeed, a delicious meal waited for Erin.

She cursed under her breath feeling taken advantage of. Using the couch for leverage, she slowly got to her feet. She clung to the couch for dear life as her world spun and darkened. She gritted her teeth and willed herself to remain conscious. When the darkness faded, and the world stopped spinning like a drunken top, Erin shuffled to the kitchen where her dinner had already been laid out for her. It was a simple fair, but she didn't care. It could have been a can of Fae's cat food; she would have eaten it just as ravenously.

The food gave her enough strength to tackle the stairs so she could get a better quality of rest.

The next morning, Erin woke with no lasting effects from the day before. She got dressed and went to work. Although she probably could have taken the remainder of her leave, it helped her to have something to distract her from the looming battle. That night, she and Fae returned to the astral plane to forge another piece of armor. This piece would be made from the bracelets chosen by the twins. Instead of casting them into the fire together, Erin did them one at a time. The silver bracelet became a set of arm guards and the gold bracelet became shin guards. Sweating profusely, Erin surveyed her work. She now had a helmet, chainmail, arm and shin guards. She had one last piece to make. She took the dagger and tossed it into the flames. Even though she knew she was nearing her breaking point, Erin felt compelled to continue. Her world zeroed in on the shapeless glob she pulled from the fire. With each strike of her hammer, another piece of the outside world faded away until there was nothing left but her and the glowing mass on the anvil before her. She felt herself pour more and more of her power into it until nothing was left but a small silvery pool of power surrounded by darkness. Erin started to reach for that silvery pool until she heard her ancestors cry out as one.

"NO!"

The cry startled Erin enough to shake the hold the magic had over her. The fact that she had come so close to losing herself to the call of magic chilled her to the core.

Erin stepped back from the shimmering chest plate on the anvil. There was no need to put it in the cooling trough. Erin took a step back, breathing heavily. Fae sat quietly on his perch. She wasn't mad at him for not stopping her. He had already warned her once, and she hadn't heeded it. It was Fae's job to guide and teach Erin what she needed to know, and sometimes, students had to learn things the hard way—and learned her lesson she had.

She stared at the glowing piece of armor still resting on the anvil. With slightly trembling hands, Erin picked it up and added it to the rest of her armor. It was now complete. Without a word, Erin gathered up Fae and fled back to the physical world, where she spent several days coming to terms with her most recent brush with death. This one shook her more than all the others because she almost killed herself, and she hadn't even been trying to.

Three days later, Erin received a package in the post. She was perplexed until she saw the return address. It came from the Fairmont family. This package was the first boon to arrive. She tore into the package, spilling the contents onto the table—a bronze arrowhead and tiny acorn. Inside was also an envelope that instructed Erin to combine the two items together. Erin debated waiting for the other boons to arrive but decided against it. She would need time to practice with the weapons, and she didn't want to have a repeat of the chest plate incident.

Back at the forge, Erin threw the arrowhead and acorn into the fires. They turned into two molten blobs. Erin watched fascinated as the blobs flowed over the hot coals like mercury, merging into one blob that stretched out into a shaft the size of her forearm. Erin pulled the shaft out and began the forging process. Once it was all said and done, Erin was left holding a long spear. There was nothing elegant about the spear; the shaft was made of wood, most likely oak, and the spearhead was made of iron, but beneath the surface, Erin could feel power coursing through it. Amazed, she placed the spear into one of the racks so it could finish settling into its new form.

It was like that first boon opened the floodgates because every day after that, Erin received another package bearing a boon from one of her allies. The hedge witches had sent theirs together, naturally. Their boons consisting of a simple dirk and ancient-looking silver coin that when reforged became a short sword and a shield. Erin was surprised to see that both items bore a wolf motif in honor of Erin's family heritage.

Mark the healer sent a charm with a symbol that Erin didn't recognize carved onto it. When Erin was done working with the strange coin, it had become a set of armor for Fae. His armor protected his vulnerable parts—throat and underbelly. Fae preened in his new armor, purring loudly.

Ylanna's boon came next. Erin already knew what it was. When she called the seer, Erin gave her a specific request. Inside the embroidered bag was a variation of the herb bundle she used against the witchlings Connor sent after her. Because of the changes Erin made, she hadn't quite felt comfortable creating the bundle herself. Ylanna with her vast knowledge and skill was better suited for the task.

Even though no one would hold it against her, Erin didn't want to kill Connor. She didn't want to stoop to his level. If she was left with no alternative, she would, but until then, she would do everything within her power to avoid taking a life.

Time continued its march forward until Erin was left with only two weeks left before the full moon and her final confrontation with Connor. She was starting to get worried. Had she prepared enough? Would her plan work? Where in the world was Eulalie's boon? The voodoo priestess still hadn't responded to Erin's summons. Charlotte's boon had arrived just the day before. She sent Erin three small vials of strange liquid with a note informing Erin that the vials were battle spells ready to be used. The only thing Erin had to do was say a single word associated with each vial, and the spell would activate. Erin was glad the vials were different, or she wouldn't have been able to tell the vials apart. So, if Charlotte had sent hers, there was no good reason for Eulalie's to still be absent. The woman owed Erin a debt but wasn't an ally. Perhaps she didn't feel the same obligation to send aid. Or maybe she was just that petty. Erin's money was on the latter.

To help distract her, Fae suggested that in order for Erin to be comfortable fighting in her new armor and using her new weapons, she needed to train with them. It made sense, and it left her too exhausted to fret over the 'what ifs' and the unknown. At first, Erin was awkward and clumsy. She spent more time picking herself off the ground than actually fighting. It didn't help that Fae thought it was best if they trained together while he was in his giant fighting cat form. Each swipe of his massive paws reverberated down to Erin's bones but left her completely uninjured. He hadn't even managed to put a scratch on her armor. Unfortunately for Erin's peace of mind, training soon lost its ability to occupy her mind.

Ye have done all that ye can, Fae told Erin as he watched her pace around her kitchen. She gnawed on her thumb until it bled. *There's nothing left ye can do but practice. I'd suggest an easy evening. Do something that will take yer mind off things. There's nothing left ye can do until ye meet Connor on the battlefield.*

Erin stopped her pacing. Her face was pale and tight. She closed her eyes and took a deep breath, willing some of her unease away. "You're right, Fae, as always."

Erin uncorked a bottle of merlot and poured herself a large glass. She then walked into the living room, trailed by Fae. She set the wine glass next to her favorite ready chair before turning to the old record player. She dug out one of her favorite albums, a soundtrack to some old movie she never heard of, and put it on. As the first gentle notes filled the air, a bit more of Erin's tension loosened. She then ran her hand, lovingly over the numerous books that lined the built-ins on either side of the fireplace. Her hand stilled over a worn book. It was the book Erin read her first night in Dorshire. Erin smiled, marveling at how much she had changed from the first time she read the book. She plucked the book from the shelf and curled up into her favorite reading chair, pulling a lap quilt over her legs to settle into a quiet night of reading, but it appeared that the fates had other ideas.

No sooner had they settled down than someone banged violently at the front door. With a shared questioning look, Fae and Erin uncurled themselves from the chair and silently made their way towards the front door. Fae's eyes glowed with his otherworldly fire while magic sparked to life at the tips of Erin's fingers. The wards hadn't warned them of this person's arrival, and from the ferocity of the knocks, it was impossible to determine whether the person on the other side was friend or foe.

Erin checked her wards and found them still standing. She didn't know what to make of that. The pounding on the door ceased. Erin crept closer, placing her ear to the door.

"You have three seconds to open this door right now, Erin!"

Recognizing the voice, Erin threw the front door open, revealing an extremely pissed-looking Amara standing on her doorstep.

"You have some serious explaining to do," Amara spat, shoving her way inside.

Erin raised her eyes towards the heavens. *Oh hell*.

ELEVEN

AMARA WAS TYPICALLY a calm person. It took a lot to make her angry. Erin had only seen Amara truly angry a handful of times but never directed at her—until now. Amara's eyes blazed. Her whole body was tense, and her movements were jerky as if she was attempting to rein in a strong desire to lash out. It reminded Erin of wild cats in captivity. As her friend paced around the foyer, Erin could only watch numbly, too taken aback by this sudden change in events. Slowly, she closed the front door. The click of the door closing caused Amara to cease her pacing and zero in on the object of her frustration and anger, Erin. Reflectively, Erin slipped into a small fighting stance, only just remembering to not summon magic. Amara was her friend, no matter how she looked at Erin, and she didn't know about Erin's secret.

"You know what I find odd?" Amara asked rhetorically. "I find it odd that my grandfather, you know the shaman, reaches out and practically orders me to come see him at his village. He only does this when he has something, when there's something big he needs to tell me. And do you know what he told me when I saw him?"

Erin shook her head, eyes wide and struggling to regain her composure. She so didn't need this right now.

Amara pursed her lips, eyes narrowing. Erin felt a chill run down her spine. Her stomach clenched as her heart sped up. She would rather face Connor with nothing than what was unfolding right now.

Amara stalked towards Erin, who reflectively backed up. "He told me that I needed to be at your side while you face a 'great darkness,' as he put it." Erin swallowed. The doorknob pressed into her back. She had run out of room. Amara stood in front of her, nose to nose, silently demanding that Erin tell her the truth. But the truth got stuck in Erin's throat. As much as she wanted to tell her best friend everything, she knew that she couldn't or risk Amara's life.

As the silence stretched between the two women, the fire in Amara's eyes dwindled and then completely went out. The tension in her body softened as her shoulders slumped under the unspoken confirmation that Erin was keeping something from her, something so big that it had drastically changed her. Amara buried her face in her hands and sobbed.

"I knew," she cried, "I knew when I visited that something had changed. I knew something had happened. I spent the whole time waiting for you to tell me because, why would you hide anything from me? Your best friend from the first time we met."

Erin reached out for Amara but stopped short. She wasn't sure how the other woman would react to her touching her at this moment. "There are rules I have to follow to keep you safe," Erin whispered. She couldn't give her friend any more than that.

"Damn the *rules*," Amara snapped, lifting her head. "We're best friends! Soul sisters! Doesn't that mean anything to you?"

Erin hung her head in guilt. "It means the world to me," she said, looking at her feet. "But this ..." she bit her lip and looked up.

Her heart ached at the hurt and betrayal in her friend's eyes. They had been through so much together, both good and bad. Plus, Amara wasn't completely unaware of the supernatural world. Her grandfather was an aboriginal shaman. She grew up with one foot in the real world and the other in the spirit world. But the wounds from Caleb's dismissal still stung, not even the connections she made in that sleepy little bayou town had irradiated all the hurt still locked inside her heart. She wouldn't be able to stand it if she lost her best friend as well.

From the back of her mind, Erin felt a small nudge, a feeling that she should give Amara the benefit of the doubt. It would be better to know the truth than to forever wonder if her friend would accept all of her.

"All right," Erin said at last. She stepped forward to grasp Amara's hands. "I'll tell you everything." She led her friend to the living room where they settled on opposite ends of the sofa.

Amara sat with her knees pulled up to her chest, arms crossed, and waited. Erin clasped her hands in her lap and looked down at them. And then she started to talk. Not once during her story did she look up from her lap. She heard Amara shift and move but couldn't bring herself to look up and see the expression on her friend's face.

She looked up only when she finished her tale, picking at her nails more nervous than she'd ever been in her life. Amara sat facing the fireplace, staring off into nothing as she processed everything Erin told her. The only sound came from the grandfather clock that ticked away each second like a drum, and still, Amara was silent.

Erin realized that she had lost her best friend. She felt her bottom lip begin to quiver as her heart crumbled. She was about to collapse into a fit of tears when a pillow hit her in the face without warning. Erin stopped crying, blinking slowly, as she stared at her friend like a deer in the headlights.

"I can't believe you are a bona fide, one hundred percent *witch* and didn't tell me the *moment* you found out!" Amara slumped back against the couch, throwing her hands into the air. "You know I love this stuff."

Erin sat shocked for a half a breath, and then she threw herself at her friend, pulling her into a tight embrace, laughing and crying at the same time. Amara wrapped her arms around Erin, and the two women laughed until their sides ached and tears ran down their faces.

"I promise to *never* keep you in the dark again," Erin swore, wiping her eyes. Her cheeks hurt from smiling so wide, but she couldn't stop. Her heart was so filled with love and relief that it felt like it could burst at any moment.

Amara playfully shoved Erin's shoulder. "You better." The smile on her face turned serious. "You need to have faith in those around you just as much as you do yourself."

Erin realized that her friend was right. Sure, some might turn their backs on her if they knew the whole story, but that didn't mean that she should cower behind a wall, never letting anyone get close to her. It would be a lonely way to live, and she was tired of being alone. It was time to tear down her walls and let the light in.

The next few weeks were the happiest in Erin's life. Brick by brick, she tore down the wall that she had erected to keep herself safe. She took Amara to the Grand Library and introduced her to Orrin and Kim. It turned out as well as she could have hoped. Soon, Amara pelted both Erin and Orrin about their brand of magic while educating them on the nuances of the natural style that her grandfather used.

Erin then took her to the place where it all started, the crumbling remains of Kieran's home. Amara treated it as reverently as any church. "It's our past that makes us what we are," she said to Erin as they picnicked under a large oak tree near the ruins. "It gives us the tools and knowledge to figure out who we are in the present, which will lead us to our future."

There was no aspect of her life that Erin didn't share with Amara. Erin delighted in the way Amara's eyes lit up when she performed small feats of magic for her, beautiful pieces with no other purpose than the simple enjoyment of doing them. Never before had Erin thought that her magic could ever be something that she enjoyed. It was always a tool to be used in the defense of others. But this playful side helped to ease the burden of being a Guardian. It helped her to see that she was more than just a shield against the dark forces in the world. Erin's only regret was that she couldn't take her friend to the astral plane and show her the mini world she'd built there. While

Amara was more sensitive to the supernatural, she didn't carry a single drop of magic in her blood. But it never seemed to bother her.

"That's all right," Amara said with a wave of her hand when Erin expressed her sympathy. "Not everyone can carry the gift. It's like how not everyone can draw or sing or be doctors." Amara winked at Erin, and the two dissolved into a fit of laughter.

"Don't you need to get back to your job soon?" Erin asked one morning.

Amara shook her head and took a sip of coffee. "Nah, I have a ton of personal days I never take, plus I'm not leaving until you kick Connor's butt deep into the ground."

"I appreciate the vote of confidence," Erin said with a laugh, "but you don't have to stay. In fact, I would feel better if you took the protection charm I made you and went back to Australia. The farther you are away from me, the safer you'll be."

Amara narrowed her eyes and pointed at Erin with her finger. "Don't push me away. It's my decision to stay by your side through this. No one in this world is ever completely safe, and I refuse to leave you alone. I know you too well. The closer you get to D-Day, the more in your head you'll get, and I cannot allow that to happen."

Erin raised her hands to placate her hot-tempered friend. She knew that it would be pointless to argue with Amara. Once she got it into her head to do something, nothing on this planet could stop her. Plus, she had more important issues to worry about, like the impending full moon and Eulalie's continued silence. If the old woman refused to send what Erin asked for, then all her planning and preparations would be for naught. Erin sent a small prayer to her ancestors, asking them to please gently nudge Eulalie to send the tribute.

Three days left.

In the early hours of the morning, when the sky was still dark, Erin awoke from her sleep to the sound of car doors slamming shut. She cracked one eye open and glared at her window. She wondered who in their right mind would think that the crack of dawn was the appropriate time for a visit. Mumbling under her breath, she rolled out of her delightfully warm bed, not bothering to throw on her robe. Fae lifted his head sleepily to watch her shuffle out of the room before nuzzling back into his pillow.

Down the stairs she went, stomping with each step. She heard voices talking softly from the other side of her door. Using her magic, she unlocked the door before she reached it and flung it wide open, ready to give the people on the other side a piece of her mind when her sleep-addled brain registered who stood on her doorstep.

"Yell later, just let us in," Erin's mother, Jessica, said bleary-eyed as she strode through the door. She dumped her bags unceremoniously onto the floor, heading upstairs. Her grandmother and sister looked just as tired as her mother. They, too, dropped their bags and headed upstairs for a few hours of rest.

Erin said nothing as she watched them trudge up the stairs with a scowl on her face. She rolled her eyes and closed the door behind her.

"Amara's asleep in the guest room," Erin called out after them.

Whether or not they heard her, Erin had no idea. She went back upstairs and crawled into her bed that she now shared with Fae and her sister. Erin yawned and smiled, bemused at the way her sister had flung herself onto the bed. She slid in between the sheets with a small sigh and fell back asleep almost immediately.

The next morning, Erin's small kitchen table was filled to capacity. The bacon sizzling in the skillet filled the air with its mouth-watering aroma, while the five women eyed the brewing coffee pot like a pack of hungry lionesses eager for the kill. Jessica, Elise, and Laura were exhausted from their international red-eye flight. Erin was slightly grumpy about her unexpected wake-up. Because of Amara's unexpected visit, she had forgotten that her family was flying out to support her. And Amara ... well, Amara wasn't a morning person in any sense of the word.

Bacon cooked to crispy perfection, Erin piled them high on a plate and placed them in the middle of the table where a heaping plate of scrambled eggs also sat, mostly untouched. "Eat up, everybody."

"Coffee first, then food," Amara grunted.

Erin chuckled and rubbed her face. "How was the flight?"

"Well enough," her mother replied. "Tried to sleep on the plane, but I couldn't get my mind to shut off." She turned to look at Elise. "Did you get any sleep, mom?"

Elise shook her head. "I closed my eyes for a while but couldn't fall asleep."

Erin shrugged. "Well, I guess that means that you all will sleep soundly tonight."

Suddenly, Laura leaped from the table, cursing, and made a mad dash for her bag that still sat in the foyer. The women at the table all watched her with confused expressions.

"I forgot to give this to you last night." Laura handed Erin a small, lumpy packed, wrapped up in brown paper and wrapped in twine. "It's from Eulalie. She drove all the way up to deliver it herself. She said it was too precious to trust to the postal service."

Erin opened the package with slightly shaking hands. Had Eulalie honored her request at last?

"She also told me to tell you that this makes her even," Laura added.

Erin made a noncommittal noise. The fewer interactions with the temperamental voodoo priestess, the better it was for her. She planned on never thinking of the wicked old woman ever again if everything worked out.

Everyone watched as the brown paper fell away, revealing a rather ordinary-looking clay jar with a cork stopper. But in her world, nothing is ever as it appears. Lightly scratched into the sides of the jar were special symbols that imbued the jar with unique properties. Properties that Erin fully intended to use in her fight against Connor.

"Be right back," she told the women cloistered in her kitchen. "Save me some coffee."

She closed her eyes and willed herself to the astral plane. Like always, she briefly stretched out her senses when she arrived at the cabin. When and only when she was sure that nothing was amiss, she walked towards the cabin, smiling down at the jar. At last, the final piece of her plan had arrived. She stored the jar in the cabin under another layer of protection. She would take no risks with it. As she exited the cabin to head back, something stirred at the edges of her senses. Something small and nearly inconspicuous sniffed at her borders, searching for any weaknesses. Erin smirked and released the sendings to guard the borders. Connor must have found out that her reinforcements had arrived and wanted to test her. Let him. He would find out soon enough just how strong Erin was.

When Erin's spirit returned to her body, the jar had vanished. "Connor knows you're here," she announced. Laura choked on the bacon she had just stuffed into her mouth. Her mother reached for her throat. Her grandmother and Amara both looked resigned and ready for a fight.

The coffee pot finished brewing with a small ding. Erin got a coffee mug and poured the steaming black, life-giving liquid into it. She stirred in creamer and took a sip, relishing the slightly bitter flavor. "I felt something sniffing around my territory in the astral plane. I released my sendings to protect the borders, especially now that the last piece has arrived." Her family didn't look any less worried. "Don't forget that the last time Connor faced us, he lost. I highly doubt that he has."

Erin toasted her family with her coffee mug and stepped aside so the others could get to it. She walked over to the table, snagging a piece of bacon from the top of the pile. Savory salt and grease replaced the coffee flavoring that lingered in her mouth. She tried to not think that this may be one of her last breakfasts. She couldn't allow those thoughts to steal away her resolve. Not only did she rely on it, but the rest of her family as well. As long as she acted like she wasn't afraid, then there would be no reason for them to be afraid either.

Once everyone had resettled around the kitchen table, it was time to get down to business.

"In two days, it will be the full moon," Erin said, trying to keep the fear from her voice. "This fight has been a long time coming."

"No kidding," Laura scoffed. Her mother shushed her.

Erin smiled at her sister. "I know." Her smile fell. "We've done all we can to prepare. There's nothing left for us to do than face Connor and finally put an end to this once and for all."

"So, what's the plan?" Amara asked.

"Connor and I will fight in the astral plane. I will fight from the Grand Library, using Freya's seal, the training sigil, to strengthen my magic and hopefully give me an edge." She looked at her mother, grandmother, and sister. "You three will wait just outside the barriers of Connor's territory to claim it for our family the moment his magic fades."

"What about me?" Amara demanded.

"You will be with me at the Library," Erin explained. "It's the safest place for you to be until this is all over." Amara nodded but didn't look pleased.

"In the astral plane, I will try to weaken Connor enough to bind and imprison his spirit there."

"How?" her mother asked.

"That's what that jar is for," Elise said.

Erin nodded. The rest of the women seated around the table looked at Erin with wide eyes. It was a clever way of stopping Connor and his family without having to resort to killing him. If Erin was able to pull it off, it would be brilliant.

"Now, once Connor is imprisoned, all the spells tied to him will stop working. I need you three to get into his home and find his workroom, more specifically, his family's book. We can use that to keep his cousin in check and perhaps deter any ideas of retaliation and finally end it all."

The women around the table nodded their heads. Erin bit her lip. There was one more aspect of her plan that she needed to tell them about, and she highly doubted it would go over well.

"There's one more thing," Erin said, and the mood in the room sank. "Should I fail, should Connor defeat me …" She had to raise her hand to silence their protests. "I would be naive to not consider my own failure. Should I fail, I name my mother, Jessica, as heir." Her words rolled through the room, filled with power. A shimmering veil settled around her extremely surprised mother.

Silence fell in the kitchen. Three of the women seated around the table stared at Erin opened mouthed, while her grandmother looked pleased.

"Laura is too young to take up the mantle," Erin explained before anyone could protest. "But you, mom, you've started to learn, and you have a strong desire to protect and nurture. That's all we're supposed to do."

Her mother's face made it seem like she wanted to argue, but she didn't. Instead, she reached across the table and gripped her daughter's hand tightly. "I don't believe you will fail. I have faith in you. But I accept all the same."

Erin hoped that by naming an heir, it would keep Connor from accessing the well pool of her family's magic, saving the rest of her family's lives. Of course, it was only a theory that she stumbled upon while digging through some crumbling scrolls in the Grand Library.

With battle plans carefully laid out and contingencies in play, all talks about magic, prophecies, and fighting ceased. The women didn't want to waste any more time worrying about them. There was nothing left for them to do now but wait. So, instead, they filled the remaining days with laughter, light, good food, and good company.

On the eve of the final confrontation, Erin wanted to host a large dinner with all her friends and family. She had already spent the better part of the day prepping the meal and calling her friends. Her house was filled to the rafters with the aroma of delicious foods and the laughter of good company.

Erin, however, found herself in town, picking up a crucial, missing ingredient and Moira—whose car was in the shop. Amara and Laura had chosen to accompany her, wanting to get out of the crowded house for a while. They stood outside Moira's nursery while she finished locking up for the day, chatting amongst each other.

Laughing at something her sister said, Erin turned and happened to glance over her shoulder. Her laughter died instantly, breath stolen and heart stilled.

There across the street, in front of the pub, stood Caleb.

Their eyes locked in on each other, and Erin felt the rest of the world fade away until it was the two of them separated by an impassable chasm.

"What is it?" Laura asked when she noted the pained expression on her sister's face.

Erin lowered her eyes and shook her head. "It's nothing."

"Isn't that the stud muffin we had drinks with that one time?" Amara pointed out.

"Yeah," Erin muttered. She looked to the heavens, seeking support. "We went out for a while," she said, her voice tight. "He ended it when he found out about ..." She waved at herself.

Laura's and Amara's eyes widened when they realized what she meant. The two women turned and glared daggers at Caleb from over their shoulders. He visibly recoiled from the intensity in their eyes. He dropped his gaze and continued his stroll down the sidewalk.

"Leave him be, guys," Erin urged. "It's over and done with. We got more important things to worry about."

Fortunately, Moira exited her shop a few moments later. Erin helped Moira with her bags, and they all piled into Erin's truck. Laura climbed into the back of the bed and spared one last glance towards Caleb who had stopped to watch Erin and the others drive off. She chewed her cheek, wondering what to do about him.

Zero hour.

The air in Erin's house was tense and filled with magical static from the nerves of four witches. No one slept because they were too nervous about the dawn and what it brought with it. Instead, the women piled around the living room. A fire burned merrily in the hearth more for comfort than for heat. Five pairs of eyes locked onto the flames, lost in their own thoughts and fears over the battle to come.

"Whatever happens tomorrow," Erin said, not taking her chin off her knees, "I want each of you to know that I love you, and I'm happy with the way my life has played out, suffering and all."

Her words broke the dam of emotions. Tears flowed freely, and the women clung to one another, eventually falling asleep in a heap together.

Hand in hand, Amara and Erin walked through the magic door to the Grand Library, with Fae trailing after them. Erin looked at the expansive knowledge cloistered around her for what could perhaps be the last time. A sense of overwhelming pride filled her as she looked out over something that would last beyond her, beyond Connor, beyond everything. If she were to die today, at least she had this one accomplishment to point to and say, "I did something with my life."

On any ordinary day, the space in the middle of the Grand Library was filled with a number of desks for study. Only when Erin helped young witches learn their spells was the floor cleared like it was now. Her eyes followed the elegant curse and subtle artistic flare of the sigil. It boosted a magic wielder's power. It also served as the strongest protection circle ever crafted. Erin hoped that it would give her an edge over Connor's years of experience and protect her friends should things not go as well as she hoped.

"Erin," Orrin said, walking out of the shadows. "The Library is closed and at your disposal."

Erin bowed low to her friend. When she straightened, she held out a large leather-bound book with a bloodstained stone set in the middle of the cover—her family's book. Orrin would hold it in confidence for her family until someone came to claim it.

Orrin bowed in return and stepped aside. Erin's world shrank to the sigil laid out in the middle of the floor. With her head held high, she strode to the center of the sigil. She turned to face her friends who tried for her benefit to look brave just like her. Fae rubbed against her ankles, letting her know that she was not alone. Erin smiled down at him, grateful for his presence and support.

Erin shifted her gaze forward and squared her shoulders. Slowly and methodically, she rolled and shook out her limbs and joints, trying to dispel her nervous energy.

She flashed her friends a half smile but knew that she couldn't keep all her fear from her face.

She saw Amara wrestle with something before she dashed towards her. Erin reached out to stop her friend. "You know you can't come with me."

Amara had tears in her eyes. "I know. I just …" She thrust something into Erin's hand—her rosary.

Erin recognized the rosary. Amara wore it almost every single day. She gave her friend a quizzical look.

"You know I've never really been much of a believer. But I've been in some hairy situations and came out all right in the end because I had this." She looked down at the rosary dangling from Erin's hand. "It may not even do anything where you're going, but I'll feel better knowing you have it. Who knows, maybe some of the luck will rub off onto you."

Erin stared the rosary and then slowly wrapped it around her wrist. When she looked up again, a few tears had broken free and fell silently down her face. She pulled Amara in one last time for a tight embrace that conveyed more than words ever could. Amara gave Erin an encouraging nod as she backed out of the sigil until she stood next to Orrin.

"Kick his ass and come back," he croaked out, his voice cracking from raw emotions. "He's always underestimated you; don't do the same."

Erin nodded once and then looked down at her familiar. "You ready, Fae?"

Fae mewed and erupted into a whirl of emerald flames, growing to the form he usually wore when it came time for a fight. Erin smiled grimly before closing her eyes and drifting into the astral plane.

TWELVE

THE TALE-TALE cool mist that swirled around her ankles told Erin that she had safely made it to her territory in the astral plane. The comforting sights of the cabin, stables, and quiet forest encircling everything greeted her when she opened her eyes. She could see Fae's fires flickering from the corner of her eye. She gave herself only a moment to orientate her senses before she strode straight to the armory to make ready for the battle.

A heavy presence hung over everything, causing the hair on the back of her neck to rise. Even the sendings who were recharging in their stalls were quite yet tense as they shuffled from one foot to the other.

In the armory, Erin found herself staring at her armor, glistening and freshly minted on its stand. Wordlessly, she slid into the chainmail shirt before reaching for the chest piece and sliding it over her head. She took comfort from the now familiar weight and feel of the armor as she bucked up the sides. The chainmail sleeves sighed with each movement of her arms. The wrist guard went on next. Erin ran her hand over the tree carved into the middle, tracing its raised edges. It only took a few moments for her to quickly lash on her leg guards.

Erin twisted and bent in her armor, ensuring that every piece moved smoothly and freely so to not impede any movement. She left the helmet, running her hand over its dome, and set to work fitting Fae into his armor.

She knelt down to fasten the neck guard around his neck, running her fingers over the same leaf motif that her armor bore. She grunted as she hoisted the spine guard up onto Fae's back. She marveled at the beauty of the scale plated armor that would not only protect her familiar's spin but also wouldn't inhibit his movements in any way. Once the top buckles were fastened, she signaled for Fae to stand so she could get to the bottom attachments. Fae performed a similar rolling dance, shifting his armor into place.

Satisfied, he walked out of the armory to perform a cursory check of the grounds before they left.

Erin felt her eyes drawn to the weapons rack. Her mouth went dry as her heart sped up. The reality of the situation all finally dawned on her. She was about to be in a magical, hand-to-hand combat with a dark practitioner who has decades of experience over her. She had to take several deep breaths to quell her rising panic. Steeling her spine, she snatched the short sword off the rack and belted it to her waist. She slid the spear behind her back before grabbing her shield. Hanging from one of the unused racks dangled a small leather pouch. Erin snatched it up and lashed it to her belt. She grabbed the embroidered bag with magic herbs and the spirit jar from Eulalie and stuffed them into it. The end of Amara's rosary swung free, catching her eye. Erin carefully tucked it back, turning to grab her helmet.

She carried it under her arm, and she walked out of the armory. Fae had already released the sending who stood silently in a row, awaiting their orders. Erin surveyed them like a commanding general inspecting her troops.

"Protect the borders of this territory at all costs," she ordered. "Let none pass except for myself and Fae. Do you understand?"

As one, the sendings bowed and drifted away to safeguard the borders of Erin's domain in the astral plane. She didn't want to be cut off from the only safe place available to her should she need to retreat.

Together, she and Fae walked down the wooded path towards the borders of her land. As the woods faded, a five-foot-tall wall came into view. Fae turned to look at his mistress with a questioning expression. Erin shrugged, nonchalant. The height was for her peace of mind, and she wouldn't apologize for it.

Erin put her helmet on. It hugged the curve of her skull perfectly, with the edges curving gracefully to protect her brow and the sides of her face. She gave Fae a short nod, letting him know that she was ready. When he nodded back, they strode through the wall together into the unclaimed lands beyond her wall.

The mists of the astral plane went on forever. In the dim light, it was hard to make out anything not two feet in front of you. Erin slowly pulled her spear free from its sheath, holding its point towards the ground, and adjusted her grip on her shield.

This was it. Go time. D-day. No more waiting.

Erin took a deep breath before she spoke. "I, Erin McManin, Guardian of the village Dorshire, challenge Connor Ferguson to open combat for the life of the land and all creatures therein."

She felt a tug near the middle of her chest just before everything rushed past her in a blur. Oddly enough, the ground beneath her feet did not seem to move, nor was there any wind, but the mists all around her streamed past at an alarming speed. She struggled not to fall over when they suddenly stopped.

The vacant mist field plane around her looked no different than the ones that surrounded her territory. The only difference was the feel of the space. An anxious dread coiled around Erin's legs, slowly inching its way up. She swore and slashed at her feet with her spear. The feeling of dread disappeared. A cruel chuckle echoed around her.

Connor walked out of the mists. His armor was reminiscing of a Roman legionary. The horizontal metal plates that made up the bulk of the armor were blacker than night itself and seemed to drink in the little bit of light that was present on the astral plane. Underneath the armor, Connor, too, wore chainmail, although his sat close to his body. He wore no leg protections at all but rather tough-looking leather pants that clung the muscles in his legs, with a pair of plain boots, also black, on his feet. Around his waist sat two modern-looking handguns. Erin thought they seemed out of place against the ancient-looking armor. Erin couldn't see a helmet; if Connor had one, he didn't bring it. Her eyes shifted to the long, twisted, black staff in his right hand. Just the sight of the wicked-looking staff caused her to break out into a cold sweat. At the staff's apex, a violet gem flickered with an otherworldly power.

Connor strode towards Erin, stopping only scant yards away. The aura of his power rippled around the edges of his body. Waves of malice, cruelty, and malevolent intentions emanated outward. They crashed against Erin's aura, leaving her feeling sick until Fae snarled, taking a single step forward.

"Tread carefully, Connor," Fae snarled. "Ignore the sacred laws of combat, and I will rip you to shreds myself and save my mistress the trouble."

Connor rolled his shoulders and head. "No need to get your fur in a bunch, *fairy*." He spat the last word out like an insult. Fae bared his teeth, a deep growl rumbled in his chest. Erin shifted closer to her familiar, pressing her body against his. Connor was trying to goad Fae into violating the laws himself. Her touch stilled the giant flaming feline, and though he backed down, the rumbling in his chest continued. Connor snickered.

"Either accept the challenge or step down and admit defeat," Erin shouted, pointing her spear point at Connor. "Enough stalling; this fight has been a long time coming."

Eyes as cold and hard as ice snapped up to meet hers. Erin didn't flinch. She was past flinching. "Too right you are," Connor agreed slowly. He stood tall and banged his staff against the invisible ground. Thunder rolled around the two magicians.

"I, Connor Ferguson, keeper of my family's name, accept the challenge for dominion of these lands and therein by trial of direct combat."

He banged his staff three more times, each one followed by a peal of thunder. From the mists, three gigantic humanoid shapes rose and lumbered a few awkward steps forward—sendings.

Erin shifted into a fighting stance, holding her shield slightly up, ready to protect, and her spear at the ready. All mirth faded from Connor's face to be replaced by a cruel sneer. This was Connor's true face, the one he kept hidden from the world.

His lip curled as the violet gem on top of his staff began to pulsate like a heart. "Last chance to surrender, Guardian."

Erin responded by encasing her body in a shield of white light edged with gold. Fae responded in kind, fully engulfed by his emerald flames.

"So be it."

He struck without warning. Connor whirled his staff towards Erin, sending a wave of black fire that she blocked just barely in time. The force of the blow reverberated through her shield down her arm all the way up to her shoulder.

Fae roared and leaped to defend his mistress but was met by all three of the sendings. In a blur of flame, shadow, and claws, they crashed into the ground, rolling and snarling and slashing as they went. They eventually disentangled, the three sendings circling Fae. Erin spotted three bloody slashes along his flank, just below his armor. Fae roared again, shooting a whirling stream of green fire at the nearest sending. It screeched its inhuman cry, curling in on itself in an attempt to quell the flames.

Another shot of black fire brought Erin's attention back to her opponent. She cursed herself for becoming distracted.

"Let the beasts fight amongst themselves," Connor said before releasing another volley of attacks in the form of fiery orbs.

Erin managed to get her shield up in time for each volley, but each impact caused her to slide back. She gritted her teeth as she searched desperately for an opening to lash out and stop the barrage of fireballs thrown at her.

"So, after all this time, *this* is the best you have to offer," Connor sneered; he swung his staff, releasing another wave of black fire. "All this planning on your part and your ancestors ... how pathetic."

Seething, Erin swatted the last of the flames aside, thrusting her spear forward at the same time with a shout. Golden energy built at the tip of the spear briefly before blasting towards Connor. Erin watched the golden beam of light stream through the air to only be absorbed by Connor's magical barrier. Cursing, she unleashed a volley of attacks of her own. Spell after spell, blast after blast was absorbed by Connor's barrier. He laughed at her attempts to break it, which only fueled her rage.

Connor swung his staff, sending a wave of power that sent Erin flying through the air.

She landed with a crunch, rolling as she went. When she regained her feet, she brandished her spear to only discover that it had been broken in two during her fall. She flung it out into the mists and gasped as a sharp pain erupted from her left side. Gasping, she wrapped her free arm around her middle.

Connor strode towards her as calmly as if he was strolling through the park. With no emotion on his face, he pulled one of his guns free from its holster, pointing it directly at Erin's head. "Shame." He pulled the trigger the same time Erin held out her hand.

The shot from the gun reverberated in Erin's ears.

The sounds of Fae's battle with the sendings faded away to nothingness.

Time slowed as she watched the bullet erupt out of the barrel, streaming directly at her. She watched as it desegregated against her magical shield.

Erin released the breath she hadn't realized she had been holding. Time returned to its normal flow, and the sounds of fighting filled her ears once more. Before Connor could recover, she thrust her hand forward again, pushing a wave of pure energy at Connor, sending him sliding away from her. Gasping and exhausted, she used a few seconds of her respite to quickly check on how her familiar fared.

Nearly all of Fae's exposed body was covered in gouges and other injuries, but still, he fought on. One of the sendings had been destroyed, although he was still outnumbered. Erin briefly wondered how much longer they could hold out. She, too, was covered in small injuries. Her armor was scorched back in most places, and her shield was ready to give way at any moment. Her only consolidation was that Connor bore a few injuries from her and was quickly losing his icy composure.

Staggering back to his feet, Connor's handsome face had twisted into something dark and ugly. A single red line ran across his cheek, marring his features.

Fae's triumphant roar blasted through the calm in the fight. Both Erin and Connor turned to see the last two sendings disintegrate in emerald flames. Limping but still determined to fight, Fae slowly made his way towards Erin. Now it was two against one.

"No," Connor snarled viciously. "I will not be defeated by the likes of *you!*" He banged his staff against the ground once more, and five fresh sendings rose from the mists, cutting Fae off from joining Erin. Horrified, she watched as they all converged on her feline friend, his massive form disappearing beneath their shadowy bodies.

Screaming in anguish and anger, Erin unsheathed her sword, brandishing it at Connor. At the sounds of her anguish, his cool, calculating nature returned. He smirked and drew a strange, glowing sigil in the air in front of him.

Erin didn't recognize the sigil, and she didn't care. She charged towards her foe with a war cry, savage and strong. She reached him just as he finished drawing the sigil. She swung her sword at the sigil at the same time Connor activated it. The two opposing forces created a backlash that caused a terrible explosion of light that sent the two combatants flying through the air in opposite directions.

Connor's staff exploded from the force of the explosion when he tried to shield himself from the explosion. Erin impacted the ground with enough force to knock the air from her lungs and sent her remaining weapons scattering into the unknown. Connor painfully got to his feet, cradling a blackened hand to his chest. He coughed and spat out blood.

"Seems like you've lost your weapons," he jeered.

Erin groaned as she rolled over, going to all fours. "I don't need them to finish you," she gasped. She knew her words sounded full hardy, but she refused to give Connor any satisfaction.

Swaying on his feet, Connor summoned a wall of fire. "We'll see."

With a surprising amount of force, he thrust the inferno at Erin. She poured everything she had left into a magical shield. The wall of flames parted before her like Moses at the Red Sea. Distracted by keeping the flames from engulfing her, Erin failed to notice the secondary spell Connor wove.

She only had a brief moment between the end of the firewall and the new attack, glowing arrows, to gather her strength and go on the defensive. With a single swipe of her arm, she deflected a number of the energy arrows while using her other hand to draw a sigil of her own in the air. The sigil flashed copper before fading away. Scant moments later, dozens of thick roots burst from the mist-covered ground near Connor's feet. The roots spiraled up his leg, binding them together. Two more roots burst out, seizing his arms. Connor struggled against the roots but was unable to get free of them or summon any spell to break free.

The roots were wound up to his neck when Erin heard Fae's strangled cry from somewhere beneath the swarming bodies of the sendings. Her focus wavered, giving Connor the window he needed to break free from her bindings. He flung a black ball of energy at Erin who no longer had the energy to react fast enough. The black fire struck her squarely in the chest, and if she hadn't been wearing armor, she knew that it would have killed her.

Her entire body seized up as she fell to the ground. Unable to break her fall, unable to cry out, unable to do anything, she watched Connor stalked towards her with a triumphant smirk on his face. From the corner of her eye, she saw the sendings retreat back into the mist, leaving a heavily bleeding Fae in their wake. Erin tried and failed to summon any of her lingering magic. She was completely cut off and entirely at Connor's mercy.

Connor squatted near her, removing her helmet, throwing it carelessly off to the side. Erin couldn't speak, but she let her eyes blaze with all the hatred she felt for the man before her. Connor reached out and brushed a stray strand of hair from her face.

"It's a shame really. All that training and frantic scrambling you did trying to outsmart me, to outlast me. Turns out it was all for naught." Connor's triumphant smile takes a melancholy turn. "I take no pleasure in killing you … well, perhaps just a little. You are perhaps the one person in this world who could actually match me in intellect and power. If you hadn't foolishly followed your family's pathetic attempt to destroy mine, you might have lived a little longer."

He waved his hand over Erin's head, and she realized he had given back her ability to speak. He undoubtedly expected her to beg for her life. There was no way she would ever do that.

"You put me through hell just to get me here. You kidnapped my mother and sister. I wouldn't even be here right now if you weren't so power hungry, and it's that hunger that will be the end of you."

Connor huffed and stood up. "You had something I wanted," he said with a shrug. "How was I to know you act so rashly?" He shrugged again before taking three steps back. He began to chant under his breath, waving his hands around in the air around him. Pitch black energy swirled to life around him. Faster and faster, he chanted. Faster and faster, he moved his hands until the black energy formed a swirling vortex of night. He raised his hands over his head, sparing Erin one last parting glance before plunging the energy straight at her heart.

Amara had spent the better part of an hour pacing around the perimeter of the circle. She tried to not stare at her friend's motionless body that stood as still as a statue in the center. She stood alone since Fae was able to fully travel between the two worlds. Orrin mindlessly flipped through a book, pretending to read.

The pair tensed at the same time, turning their full attention onto the woman sealed away behind a magic barrier. Drawn by a force she didn't fully understand, Amara walked right up to the edge of the protection circle, placing her hand on the invisible wall. She felt its resistance and something else. Something that stilled her heart.

At the foot of a long gravel driveway leading up to a dark and looming castle, three women sat, poised to attack. A wind blew, stirring their hair and clothes. All three women turned to look behind them. Tears formed and fell as the women clung to each other for support. A beloved granddaughter, daughter and sister was about to be lost to them forever. Though tears fell freely from Laura's eyes, a vengeful fire erupted to life as she made a silent promise to avenge her sister.

Safely tucked away in a man-made jungle, Moira struggled to keep her hands and mind occupied. She tried and failed to not think about the young woman who fought for the sake of the place she had come to love. Suddenly, Moira gasped, dropping the pot she had been holding. Shards and dirt lay unheeded at her feet as she raised a hand to her mouth.

Caleb jerked violently out of his slumber, looking about his bedroom, drenched in sweat. His heart filled with dread as he realized what could have woken him.

Back at the Library, Amara had begun to beat against the barrier that prevented her from reaching her best friend. "Don't you do it," she shouted as she beat her fists bloody against the barrier. "Don't you bloody give up on me! Fight back, dammit! There are people who love and depend on you! Get your bloody ass back up and fight back!"

Erin heard a sound like the beating of a drum and shouting. The words of her best friend become clearer as she focused on them. Gritting her teeth, Erin dug deep inside of herself until she reached the silvery pool that was her life force. All her plans had failed because she was not strong enough. But the fight wasn't over yet. She was willing to give every last ounce of herself to protect the people she loved. Drawing from the pool, Erin regained control of her limbs, but she could feel her life dwindling. Once she was free, Erin knew that she would only have a few precious breaths to capture Connor's soul before becoming a spirit herself.

Erin sent a wave of love out to everyone who she held dear in her heart. Even those whom she would never meet and those who broke her heart. She smiled as an image of each person came and went before her eyes, and she realized what life truly was; meetings and partings. Life was about the people you met. It was about friends, family, acquaintances, loves, and heartaches. The essence of all the people that Erin had come across surrounded her and made her feel less alone as she slowly died.

At last, her arm was freed from Connor's control. She lifted it to reach for the small bag at her side that carried the bundle and jar that would steal Connor's spirit from his body and imprison it. As she reached, something swung free from her wrist—the end of Amara's rosary. It flared to life, surprising both Connor and Erin as it eradicated the swirling mass of death and broke his hold over Erin's body.

"You *dare* to bring that here, into our most sacred of places?" Connor hissed. Never before had he regarded Erin with such contempt or hatred on his face. "You dare wear a relic of the people who killed hundreds of ours!"

The end of the rosary continued to glow, and in its light, Erin felt her strength return to her as her life force filled the pool, and her magic returned. In that light, she felt the love of her family and friends, reminding her that she was not alone. Slightly unsteadily, Erin rose to her feet. She could do this.

Connor snarled and flung a black ball of energy at her. Once again, the rosary dissipated it. Connor then switched tactics and began to draw a complicated sigil in the air. Erin used the lack of his undivided attention to unwrap the rosary from around her wrist. Swinging it like a lasso, Erin tossed the rosary at Connor. She had no idea if it would work like she hoped, but she was out of options at this point. The surge of energy she initially felt was quickly fading. She had to bind him and soon.

The rosary grew as it flew through the air, transforming into a golden length of rope. Connor realized what Erin had done too late to stop it. The half-formed sigil faded back into oblivion as the golden rope wrapped its way around Connor, turning him into a glowing mummy.

Fae stirred back to life, much to Erin's delight. Slowly, he limped over to his mistress, leaning heavily against her. Beaten and bloodied, he gave what power he could so Erin could finally bring this centuries-long conflict to an end.

Erin removed an embroidered bag from the leather bag at her side and tossed it at Connor's feet. A black, shadowy chain spewed from the bag, lashing about like a living thing. One by one, the chains replaced the golden rope until nothing of Connor could be seen but his eyes; eyes that now burned with such intensity that Erin knew if she failed, she would die in the most painful of ways. But the chains didn't fail, and soon after, even Connor's eyes were covered by the shadowy chains.

Then the screaming started.

Terrible, blood-curdling screams that Erin forced herself to face. Though her throat turned dry, and her knees buckled, she did not turn away from the suffering she was inflicting. She would face the horror she created to remind herself to always choose this path as a last resort. She never wanted to forget.

After what seemed like an eternity, the screaming stopped. The chains evaporated into the mists around her, revealing the end result—Connor's soul. He was transparent and nearly disappeared in the mists of the astral plane. His soul rippled and shimmered like water. He stood emotionless and soundless, staring at Erin without seeing her. She felt sick to her stomach, but there was no going back now.

Once more, Erin reached into her pocket and pulled out a jar with strange symbols carved into it. She uncorked the jar and held the opening towards Connor's glowing form. In a flash of light, Connor's essence, his soul, his magic was sucked into the jar. Erin placed the cork back into the jar's opening and drew the rune for sleep on it with her finger. The rune shimmered on the jar for a brief moment before fading into the jar, ensuring that Connor would never awaken from his slumber.

Erin's knees finally gave out, and she fell to the ground. She clutched the jar tightly with both hands and stared vacantly ahead. She had done it. She had actually pulled it off. Her family's war was over. They had won. Before Erin could start laughing hysterically, Fae dropped the rosary into her lap, causing her to jump and bringing her back to herself. Fae sighed and fell to the ground, shrinking to his usual appearance. He had nothing left to give.

Erin scooped up her unconscious familiar into her arms, cradling him against her chest. She carefully tucked the jar back into its bag and stood up. She swayed on her feet but remained standing. It took longer than she liked to admit to travel back to her territory. She placed the jar containing Connor's soul back into the protective casing she used to safeguard the jar and then walked back outside.

Standing in the middle of her territory, Erin used the last vestiges of her will to return to the physical world.

Amara and Orrin were still pressed against the protection circle when Erin returned to her body. They breathed a small sigh of relief when they saw her and Fae in her arms. Their relief turned to alarm when Erin's body and mind finally gave out on her, and she crumbled to the stone floor. Amara and Orrin cried out to her, pushing harder against the barrier until it gave way under their fingers and they rushed to aid their battle-weary comrades.

THIRTEEN

PAIN ERUPTED FROM behind Erin's eyelids as light from the sun warmed her face. Suppressing a groan, she rolled out of the patch of sunlight to save her sensitive eyes from further onslaught from the light. Face buried into something soft and squishy, she breathed deeply. The familiar scent of lavender and the cool, crisp sheets around her bruised and battered body confirmed that she had, in fact, won the battle against Connor. She cracked open an eye, taking in the welcomed sights of her bedroom. Slowly, she eased up onto her elbows. She had no memory of how she got home. She was just happy that she was.

Turning her head caused her entire body to cry out in pain, followed rapidly by rolling bouts of nausea. When the world stopped spinning, and her stomach no longer threatened to empty whatever was left in it, Erin opened her eyes again. The pillow next to her was empty. Her mouth turned sour as her heart jumped into high gear. Where was Fae?

Fighting against the protests from her body, Erin tried to roll out of her bed.

"Oh please don't do that, sweetie," her mother pleaded as she walked in bearing a tray loaded with food and medicines.

Erin settled back against her pillows with a huff. "Where's Fae?" she croaked.

Her mother smiled and crossed the room. "He's fine. He told me to tell you not to fret."

Erin studied her mother skeptically. Her mother sighed, placing the tray on the bed. "He *was* badly injured after the battle. He said that he needed to be among his people to heal. He should be back in a day or two."

"Well, that's a relief."

Erin's mother took her hand and kissed the back of it lovingly. She beamed at Erin proudly until her eyes filled with tears. She gripped Erin's hand, white-knuckled.

"Don't you *ever* scare me like that again. Do you understand me, young lady?"

"Yes, ma'am," Erin replied, swallowing against the tightness in her throat.

Appeased, her mother turned her attention back to the tray she brought in. Erin peered at the tray and saw a number of herbs used in healing as well as a steaming teapot. Her mother busied herself with making a remedy for Erin, which undoubtedly would taste god awful.

As she waited, Erin's thoughts turned back to the final moments of her battle against Connor. She would never forget the sound of his screams for the rest of her life. Even now, tucked safely in her bed, with her mother sitting at its foot, a chill ran down her spine. She shuttered.

"You've been out for a couple of days," her mother said as if she hadn't seen her daughter's shiver. "I'm glad you're awake, but you need to take it easy and regain your strength slowly." She handed over a steaming cup of herbal tea that smelled like a mixture of dirty gym socks and honey.

Erin's nose wrinkled against the stink. The corner of her mother's mouth twitched.

"Take your medicine, or you won't get any dessert later," her mother teased.

Erin rolled her eyes and carefully took the hot cup from her mother. It smelled even worse up close. But there was nothing she could do; closing her eyes, she drank the remedy as fast as she could. Her head swam, and her stomach rolled but only for a moment.

"I'll leave you some crackers and bring up some ginger ale later on." Her mother leaned in and kissed Erin on the forehead like she was little. "I'm so proud of you."

Erin smiled sleepily back up at her mom and started to settle back down when another thought raced through her mind. "Wait! What happened at Connor's house? Did you get the book? Did his cousin give you grief?"

Her mother held up her hand. "Rest now, questions later." She saw the expression on her daughter's face and sighed. "We got it with no trouble at all." Erin raised a brow. "Honest," her mother swore. "Get some rest, baby."

Erin wanted to argue, but whatever her mother put into her drink had already started to take effect. She was out again the moment her head hit the pillow.

She woke up later, unsure if she had slept for a few hours or days. The light streaming in from her window hinted at twilight, but that was it. She slowly eased her body up, already noting an improvement from before.

"There's sleeping beauty," Amara teased from her seat in the corner of the room. She stood and placed the book she had been reading on the seat. Like her mother had, Amara latched onto Erin's hand and fought back tears.

"I heard you," Erin confessed, tearing up herself. "When I thought I was going to die, I heard you." She paused to swallow back the emotion rising in her throat. "Thank you for not giving up on me."

From the folds of her blanket, Erin pulled out the rosary that saved her life, looking as inconspicuous as before. "It saved my life in the end."

Amara let out a wet chuckle. "I told you it was lucky." She dissolved into a fit of laughter that Erin joined in on. The two women clung to one another, laughing until tears streamed down their faces and they were gasping for breath.

"So can you fill me in on what happened while I was out?"

Amara stretched out at the foot of Erin's bed. "Your mother told us not to, didn't want to distract from your recovery."

"But you won't until you know everything," Laura interjected from the doorway. When she saw her sister sitting up in bed, Laura launched herself across the room. She crashed into Erin, burying her face into her neck. Erin wrapped her arms as tightly around her younger sister as she could.

Eventually, Laura gave her sister some room to breathe, arranging her long limbs so that she sat cross-legged on the bed.

"We felt when you were about to die," Laura said. "But you didn't, so that's nice." She played with the ends of her hair while she got her emotions under control. "You should have felt the collapse. The aura around his house was terrible, even worse than Sébastien's shack." Laura shuttered. "But then, all of a sudden, there was like this big whoosh, and it was gone."

Erin made herself comfortable while she listened to her sister's tale.

The whoosh Laura had described had actually been more like a wave of malevolence being released from a dam. Laura and her mother crouched to the ground to protect themselves while Elise stood her ground against the onslaught of evil. It parted around all three like they weren't even there. It had been the most terrifying two minutes of Laura's life. Even being kidnapped by an evil voodoo king hadn't been as scary.

In the silence that fell after the wave, Laura and her mother stood up carefully. The air was clean and sweet, yet somehow vacant as if the land was waiting for someone to claim it.

"Come now," Elise urged. "We must be quick before Xander has a chance to reclaim this land for the dark."

The three women trotted up the long driveway, stopping only when they reached the massive wooden doors that would lead them into the bowels of Connor's former lair. What evils or horrors would greet them?

Cautiously, they entered the dark castle, only to find it completely empty. The only thing they saw was ancient and expensive-looking pieces of artwork and furniture.

Laura's mother pulled out a feather and spoke a strange word. The feather transformed into a tiny glowing replica of a starling, the bird the feather came from. "Find it," commanded her mother.

They chased the glowing bird down a series of tunnels that led to what had once been the dungeons. The air retained its oppressive nature, making all three women break out into a cold sweat. The farther down they went, the colder it became until they could see their haggard breaths in front of them. More than once, one of them slipped on water or moss.

The glowing sterling stopped in front of a fortified door, the only door they had passed for some time. A flickering light shone out from the bottom crack. The sterling faded back into a feather that floated gently to the damp stones.

It was Laura who reached for the doorknob and opened the door. A half-formed spell blossomed on her tongue, filling her mouth with power, causing her teeth to ache, but she held it there. She would either release it or finish casting it, depending on what she saw on the other side of the door.

Her eyes were instantly drawn to a figure sitting in a large wing-back chair, staring intently into the flames from the fire.

Xander did not acknowledge the three women who filled into his cousin's most guarded of spaces. He didn't see their eyes sweep the room for threats, didn't see the horror on their faces as they took in the number of spell books stolen through murder that lined both sides of the fireplace. The only thing he saw was the flames as he ran his hands over a large leather-bound book in his lap. He knew why they were there. He wondered if his cousin had suffered like he had made so many others suffer. He wondered why he was still alive.

Elise and Laura shared a quick glance before summoning their magic.

"Wait," Laura's mother said, taking a step forward.

It was then that Xander turned to face them. Silent tears ran down his face. He didn't look angry or sad. He looked defeated.

"I never got to choose anything in my life," he confessed to them. "From the moment my parents discovered I had magic, they shipped me off to live with Connor, claiming that it would be a great honor. If you think Connor is bad, you should have met his father. Everything that Connor is, he learned from his father, who learned from his father, and so on. I never wanted any of that."

Laura's mother knelt next to Xander and placed her hand on his arm.

"He's dead, isn't he?"

"Not quite," her mother said.

"What's going to happen to me now?"

Her mother reached up and brushed a stray strand away from Xander's face. "Whatever you want, as long as you leave us in peace. You can finally live your life."

Xander smiled. It was a true smile, one entirely his own. "I'd like that."

Erin sat stunned when Laura finished her story. "What happened to all the books? Where's Connor's family book?"

"Orrin took care of them all," Amara said. "Some of the books had a dark aura around them, so he put them in special boxes until they leveled out or something to that effect. As for the rest, he documented them and added them to the Library."

"And Connor's family's book?"

"That one he placed in a chest made of ash, oak, and hawthorn. He said that it was too dark to be handled. Perhaps it will be locked away until it turns to dust."

Erin sat back against her pillows, relieved that Orrin had handled the books for her. "Here's hoping. We still should keep an eye on Xander, just to make sure."

Amara and Laura shifted in their spots. "That's something you'll have to take up with your mother," Amara said with a look that told Erin to prepare for a fight if she did.

Erin sighed and closed her eyes. She was tired again. She fell asleep to the gentle conversations between her sister and her best friend as they talked about mundane things. Erin had never been so grateful for mundane conversations.

The next two days followed a similar routine. Erin would wake up and be forced to down some nasty concoction that knocked her out again. When she woke later on in the day, food would be provided, maybe even a bathroom trip. But on the whole, she remained confined to her bed to the point that Erin felt like a horse chomping at the bit. It was only after a *slightly* heated debate that Erin finally got her wish and got out of bed.

"For the last time, stop worrying over me," Erin snipped at her mother when she wobbled a bit, walking around her room. "I'm a Guardian *and* the head of this family. I don't need to be coddled."

Her mother huffed and crossed her arms. "I gave birth to you. Mother trumps Guardian every time."

Erin tried to argue, but nothing came to mind. Laura and Amara were no help either, cackling like a pair of wicked witches. To salvage the remainder of her dignity, Erin walked as straight as she could to the bathroom, slamming the door behind her.

She could still hear her sister and best friend laughing at her through the door. Erin tried to stay angry, but she, too, laughed at her mother's audacity.

It took only a matter of minutes for her clothes to end up discarded on the bathroom floor while she waited for the steaming water to fill the tub. Although she was in better shape than before, she still had quite a bit of healing left to do. Every muscle in her body felt like it had been replaced with boards. Her joints had swollen to the size of softballs—all right, that was an exaggeration, but they felt like it.

Erin didn't wait for the tub to fill up completely. Three-quarters full, and she clamored over the edge of the tub and lowered her aching body into the water. A loud moan escaped her mouth as the near-scalding water eased its way into her stiff and achy body. She tilted her head back so that it rested on the rim of the tub and closed her eyes, savoring the warmth.

She must have fallen asleep because her sister was pounding on the bathroom door and the water had cooled.

"You're not a mermaid," Laura shouted through the door with a chuckle. "Dinner's ready."

"Be right out," Erin shouted back. In rapid time, thanks to her newly loosened limbs, she scrubbed and got dressed. She pulled on the warmest pair of pajamas she could find and then shuffled down the stairs for dinner.

Dinner was a simple affair, and Erin was grateful that no one questioned what happened during her fight with Connor, although she would have to tell them eventually. For now, however, they caught up on the little aspects of their lives, clinging desperately to a sense of normalcy.

The next day, Erin wandered from room to room aimlessly. She didn't know where to go or what to do; nothing tickled her fancy, and she was still on the mend. By mid-morning, she had taken refuge in the study, hoping to get a handle on her new situation.

Her ancestor Kieran's prophecy had come to be and passed with Erin as the victor. Centuries of planning and fighting had cumulated to a single moment, and now that moment had passed, she didn't know what to do.

Swiveling her chair around, she turned to face the numerous accounts of her ancestors. They all lived full lives under the shadow of the prophecy. No matter what road they chose to walk, that was always their destination. But her family was free from that. What was their purpose now? Were they just supposed to wander aimlessly until there was no one left? Erin hoped not.

She turned away from the journals and reference books to pull a large book with a stone in the center out of a drawer. She ran her hands over it much like Xander did before he relinquished his past to have a future. Erin knew that wasn't an option for her family. Their magic still ran strong in their bloodline as did the desire to help those around them.

Erin opened the book and flipped through the pages absentmindedly, half hoping that the book would reveal what she needed to know like it had so many times before. Not this time. She looked at all the knowledge her family gathered to protect the land and to fight the coming of the dark family. It boggled her mind that not one of them had thought about a time after. Perhaps they felt like they didn't need to because they still had their duties as Guardians, but Erin and her family were different from these ancient Guardians.

They could not sit idly by and watch while injustices were being committed. They would not eradicate someone just because of who their family was because one's family does not dictate who you are. You can still be your own person if given the chance. They wanted to help all peoples, be they magical or not. They didn't believe in the ridiculous class systems of old. Erin straightened in her chair. They were a new breed of Guardians. They were one of the last full magical families in the world. They could bring their community out of the old ways so that it could continue to survive.

Erin smiled, filled with a new sense of purpose. She picked up her family's book and kissed the stone. In the middle of the bookcase, right at eye level, sat an empty glass box. Erin lifted the lid and gently placed the book inside. She closed it and walked out feeling sure of herself for the first time in days. Later that evening, she gathered her family around her to discuss their future and what a future it would be.

"I really think I should stay a little while longer," Erin's mother said for the fifth time. She rubbed her hands anxiously together as she watched her eldest daughter put a load into the washer.

Erin restrained her sigh. She knew her mother meant well, but now it was time for everyone to go back to their normal lives, including her mother.

"Mom, I'll be fine. I'm a grown woman, remember. I *have* to get back to my students. I undoubtedly have a literal mountain of paperwork to sift through and curriculums to catch up on. Laura's got school. Amara has her work, and you and Gran have your lives to get back to."

"You are my daughter and that takes precedence over all others," her mother argued.

This time, Erin did sigh. "Mother, I have friends here to help me if I need them. Don't make me give you an order."

Her mother opened her mouth to argue but stopped when she saw her daughter's face. It was the face of a leader. She swallowed the words she had been about to utter and walked out of the laundry room to pack.

Erin leaned up against her washer, guilt washing over her. She hated pulling rank on her mother, but it did have its merits ... sometimes. Everyone needed to start walking their own paths, her mother included, and they couldn't accomplish that if they were too afraid to take the next step.

It took two cars to get everyone and their things to the train station. Erin's grandmother and mother rode with Moira in her butter-yellow hatchback. Amara and Laura rode with Erin who had all the bags in the bed of her truck.

"I'll come for a visit during the holidays," Erin promised her mother. That seemed to ease her mother's hurt at being sent away.

Hugs, tears, and promises to stay in contact more were abundant and continuous until it was time for the passengers to board the train. Erin embraced her family and Amara one last time before waving goodbye on the platform with Moira.

Moira turned to Erin, looping her arm through hers. "I'm proud of you, birdie."

Erin patted the older woman's hand, placing her head on top of hers. "I'm proud of me too."

Moira honked when she turned off the road that would take her home. Erin honked back and drove on. She let her mind wander, going over the events of the past month. She also worried about Fae. He still hadn't returned. She hoped that his injuries hadn't been too severe. She made a mental note to go to the astral plane as soon as she was able and see if she couldn't contact him. Just because she had fulfilled the prophecy didn't mean that she didn't want or need her familiar any less.

Erin frowned at the unfamiliar car in her driveway. She wasn't expecting any visitors. She had been looking forward to having the house to herself again. She pulled around the car to park in her usual spot. She groaned getting out of her truck, as she was still recuperating, and walked over to the car to see who it was. She felt no fear at the sight of the unfamiliar car. She had defeated her greatest enemy and knew down to the marrow of her bones that she could handle whoever was sitting in the car.

The person in the other car opened the door and got out. All of Erin's confidence went straight out the metaphorical window. She latched onto the side of the truck's bed to keep her legs from giving way.

Caleb had come to visit her.

Time stretched on while the two former lovers stared at each other. He looked much the same as the last time she had seen him up close. His brown hair was a little shaggier but still suited him. His warm eyes scanned every inch of her body as if searching for signs of injury.

Erin felt her cheeks heat up, and she let out a small cough. Caleb blushed and met her eyes, but the silence continued.

"I have been an utter prick," he muttered at last, breaking the silence.

Erin felt the corners of her mouth twitch. She thought it would be best to wait and see where that particular line of conversation went.

Caleb ran his hand through his hair. "I don't blame you in the slightest for keeping your magic a secret, especially after what your sister told me."

Erin's amusement turned to dread so fast that her vision darkened around the edges. Laura had spoken to Caleb! When? Why? She swore to kill her sister the next time she saw her.

"Just what *did* my sister say?"

Caleb looked up at Erin with a sheepish smile on his face. "Everything."

Erin groaned and threw her hands up towards the heavens. Yup, she was definitely going to kill her sister. She would get on a plane tonight in fact and kill her for putting her in this situation.

This time, it was Caleb who fought to not smile. "Look, don't be mad at her. I guess she felt like I needed to know the truth ... the whole truth. If I were to be completely honest, she came up to my house and scolded me like my old school marm used to."

Erin smiled imagining an eight-year-old Caleb getting scolded by a stern-looking woman for not completing his homework.

Caleb took her smile as the okay to move forward. Erin's spine snapped ram-rod straight. He stopped.

"She really didn't have to come tell me that I was an ass. I knew that from the moment I saw you on the streets that day. What you kept hidden, you did for a reason. We had only just begun to get to know each other, and with everything that came attached to it at the time," Caleb shrugged, "it makes sense that you would keep that to yourself."

"I wanted to," Erin admitted. "I just couldn't because …"

"I know."

She smiled again, taking a few steps forward. Caleb seemed to sag with relief and met her halfway. Her whole body hummed with an overall feeling of rightness. They were meant to be together. She knew that now beyond a shadow of a doubt.

Caleb reached out and took both of Erin's hands in his. "Can you find it in your heart to forgive me?"

For a fraction of a second, Erin's heart stopped. The wind stopped. Everything stopped, and then it all came crashing back.

Caleb continued, unaware of the maelstrom of emotions he had unleashed inside Erin.

"I don't expect us to get back together or anything like that. I just want to see if there's any possible way that I can fix this rift between us. You are an amazing woman, Erin. You're funny and strong and ... You will *literally* fight for those you care about."

Erin chose her next words carefully. "You haven't messed up *that* badly."

The hopeful expression on Caleb's face made her want to throw her arms around his neck, wrap her legs around his waist and have him show her just how sorry he actually was. She shook her head. No, they needed to rebuild slowly. Lay down a better foundation, a stronger foundation—one that would never crumble again.

Caleb extended his hand. "Hi. My name's Caleb. I work for the power company. My family is too large and too pushy for their own good, but I love them all the more for it, and I can be a complete dick sometimes and overreact."

Erin extended her hand and gave him a firm shake. "Nice to meet you, Caleb. I'm Erin. I come from a long line of magical protectors. It's my sworn duty to protect those under my charge from all forms of evil influence. I'm also a teacher at a private school. My family is small but overly protective, and they don't really understand the meaning of boundaries."

Caleb returned her handshake, but she didn't let go.

"Oh, one more thing. I have a cat that's not really a cat. He's my familiar and comes from the fairy realm. He's away, healing after an epic battle that was foretold centuries ago."

The laughter on Caleb's face faded away. "How are you, really?"

"I'll be fine, been up and about for a few days now. If you want, you can come in, and I'll tell you about it."

"Sure."

Caleb followed Erin to her stoop. The day finally caught up to her, and she stumbled a bit on the stairs. He instinctively reached out to help her, causing her body to sing once more. She smiled back at him and let him help her up the rest of the stairs.

She reached for the doorknob but stopped when a strange wind blew across her property. She looked out into the distance because she would have sworn that she heard a sigh. It sounded like the type of sigh you made when everything was in its proper place and you were utterly content. Her eye was drawn to the vibrant sunset that had turned the sky into an artist's palate.

With the setting sun, one chapter of her family's history was over. One chapter of her life was over. When the sun rose anew on the following morning, a new bright chapter would begin, one whose beginnings were already in motion.

Caleb followed Erin's gaze and gave her a slightly confused look. She shook her head and motioned for him to follow. She poured them two small glasses of whiskey and posed a toast.

"To the end of a chapter and the beginning of another."

"To rebuilding what was broken," Caleb agreed.

To the future, Erin thought as she tipped the glass up.

Acknowledgments

So here we are, the ending of long, trying, but enjoying journey. There have been ups and downs throughout the writing of this story and I couldn't have done it without the support from my darling husband, who listened to me prattle on and on about the writing process while he tried to play his video games with his friends (sorry for all the times I got you killed).

And if I wasn't for Jessica Parker whose constant questioning about when my next book was coming out, I probably would have taken longer to finish. Never say that nagging doesn't get things accomplished.

I also want to thank Jenna Moreci. Your words of wisdom and hilarious truths keep me from taking myself too seriously and give me a laugh right when I need it the most.